# UNRULY CREATURES

# Unruly Creatures

—

## short stories

—

# JENNIFER

# CALOYERAS

VANDALIA PRESS

MORGANTOWN 2017

ISBN:


PB: 978-1-943665-78-5

EPUB: 978-1-943665-79-2

PDF: 978-1-943665-80-8


Library of Congress Cataloging-in-Publication Data

is available from the Library of Congress

Cover design by Than Saffel. Illustration by Bryn Perrott.

Author image: Gene Fama

"The Sound of an Infinite Gesture" appeared in *Monday Night* 11 (2012).

"Unruly" appeared in *Storm Cellar* 3, no. 1 (Fall 2013).

"Roadkill" appeared in *Wilde Magazine* 2 (Spring 2013).

"Plush" appeared in *Booth* (February 2014).

"Stuffed" appeared in *COG* 3 (Spring 2016).

# Contents

---

# The Sound of an Infinite Gesture

———

Things were getting weird in the gorilla habitat.

Last week, Conga, the three-hundred-pound Rwandan primate, one of only four gorillas in the world who could sign over five hundred words, gave the middle finger seven times to a wide-eyed group of kids who had waited over half the school year to visit the Institute for Privileged Primates.

The first flipped bird was aimed at the kids in the center of the observation window.

The second and third came in unison, arms outstretched to full wingspan, like a conductor bringing the string section to a sudden crescendo.

Number four wove under her muscular leg, a sneak attack, which seemed to be directed at the only girl in the room shielding her eyes.

Teachers, who were lined up behind their kids at the back of the room, hadn't had a moment to digest five and six before Conga built up to the grand finale, her massive hand starting out low and then rising like a rocket ship piloted by drunken astronauts.

The gorilla habitat closed for the rest of the day.

Jan should have known there was going to be trouble. On her first day working with Conga, three months ago, Yeager had flagged her down with his shovel.

"Good luck. I hear she's a real shrew."

Jan just shrugged. What did he know anyway? The proboscis monkeys he cared for had deflated ball sacs for noses. But Yeager couldn't let it go.

"She could kill you if she wanted to." He walked with a permanent wobble due to an unspoken injury.

Jan fingered the mandatory emergency clicker, clipped to her belt loop, just in case. One push of the red button would send security members to the area, all equipped with tranquilizer guns. The Institute had never had to put this plan into action, but twice a year all employees were required to take part in a rescue simulation.

But Conga didn't ever scare her—none of the apes she'd ever worked with had.

After a week of whistle training to rehabilitate Conga's misuse of her middle digits, Dr. Walker, the head of IPP, gave the *all clear* to resume school visits.

"Good morning, everyone. I'm Jan Albud and I'm Conga's trainer," Jan told the latest batch of school kids. Jan had gotten into this business to observe, not be observed, so presentation days were challenging. Besides her fellow trainers whom she rarely hung out with, these visitors were pretty much her only regular contact with humans. She spoke into the small microphone clipped to her collar as she addressed the kids through the shatterproof glass of the gorilla enclosure.

"Where's the monkey?" shouted a squat boy, his greasy nose plastered to the observation window.

"Well, she's technically not a monkey. She's a gorilla, in the *Hominidae* family and she shares over 98 percent of our DNA! If you look carefully, you'll notice she's in her favorite hiding spot. Does anyone see her?"

Voices quieted as the kids scanned the enclosure.

"Should we have her come out?" asked Jan.

The audience brought their hands together, clapping and chanting the gorilla's name in a persuasive cheer.

Jan reached into her sweatshirt pocket and pulled out a chocolate pudding cup. Within seconds the lumbering gorilla crawled out from under a trampoline and knuckle-walked right up to Jan, grabbed the snack, squeezed the container until the top popped open and downed it like a Jell-O shot. She then crushed the plastic in her fist and threw the empty container on the floor. The crowd went wild with applause.

The gorilla enclosure was divided into two sections, outdoors and indoors. Outside, the grounds were lushly overgrown, and a series of ropes, made to look like vines, were strategically placed for Conga to climb. There was a large rocky area surrounding a pool of water, where she sunned herself. Landscape architects and designers had worked hard to recreate as close to an authentic home as possible.

There was nothing natural about the indoor area, though, which looked more like a preschool than a gorilla habitat. Conga had an art nook with a sturdy chair and table set up with colorful containers filled with markers, crayons, and chalk. Construction paper was stacked in recycling bins and a roll of butcher paper lay draped over a supersized easel. The kitchen area had a faux stove, pots, pans, and empty cans and boxes of cereal all taped shut. A three-tiered basket hung from a hook filled with plastic fruit and vegetables. A group of schoolchildren from Moscow had sent Conga her own chef's hat with her name embroidered on it, which rested on a hook above the stovetop. There were mixing utensils, whisks, and even something that looked like a martini strainer. Conga had a dress-up area, a building center, beanbags, a hammock, and a reading corner packed with board books.

But Conga's favorite item was the flat-screen TV that Dr. Walker had purchased, dipping into funds allocated for the fragile spider monkeys. He said, "A TV would allow Conga to watch reality shows so that she can be hip to modern lingo. We want a gorilla who can speak to teens." So far, she had refused to watch anything other than Turner Classics, which did nothing to help her reach Dr. Walker's goal of "accelerated evolution."

Midway through the presentation, Jan was relieved that none of the kids had made references to last week's finger episode.

"How do you think you say 'banana' in sign language?"

A little girl made what could have been interpreted as a lewd gesture, her attempt at signing the fruit.

"Good guess!" Jan corrected the girl and pointed up with an index finger, then brought her other hand to the tip of her finger and pretended she was peeling a banana. The crowd tried it as well. She then taught them how to sign "apple" and "orange."

"Which fruit do you want?" Jan directed her sign to Conga, who was now spinning in circles, signing the word "dizzy."

The gorilla came to a stop, thought it over, then brought her right hand in a closed palm up to her jaw and turned it, giving the sign for apple. The children were riveted. Jan then went through a series of emotions, asking Conga how she felt today. The gorilla answered that she was tired, making a sign that looked like she was sweeping cobwebs off her thick hips.

Three lucky students were chosen to ask Conga a question, which Jan interpreted using sign language.

"What's your favorite game?" (Hide and seek.)

"Who's your best friend?" (Jan.)

"Do you have any pets?" (Yes.)

"Conga, what kind of pet do you have?" Jan signed.

Conga brought a fist to her chin and extended two fingers in a coquettish wave.

"What she's saying is that she has a frog." Jan walked past the art corner to a small terrarium sitting on the counter next to the sink. She slid the mesh covering toward her, picked up the frog, and carried it back over to Conga, who held it delicately with both hands.

"Do any of you have pet frogs?"

Six arms reached for the ceiling.

"What's its name?" A freckle-faced girl asked.

"Conga calls her 'Leg,' and you love Leg, don't you?" Jan signed as she walked toward her audience.

The presentation was almost over. All she had to do was urge them to sign an invisible petition, with their fingers in the air, to take care of the environment so that gorillas would always have a place to live and her job would be done. They'd wave good-bye and get funneled to the gift shop, where those who came prepared could shell out $100 for an original watercolor by the famous primate. Those who didn't have the money went home, at the very least, with a $3 keychain depicting Conga signing the word "Love."

"Um, what's the monkey doing?"

Jan turned around. Conga had placed Leg on the ground and was standing on her red plastic chair. As if she had been stung by a wasp, she performed a wrestling move known as the Corkscrew Splash, leaping up off the chair and spinning in a circle in the air before landing belly first. She quickly rolled aside to give her audience a peek at the animal that was no longer technically a frog, but a green Play-Doh pancake.

At the emergency staff meeting called by Dr. Walker, Jan defended Conga.

"She must have learned it from one of the kids. She was just mimicking behavior. It's in her nature." Jan momentarily missed the uncomplicated orangutans she used to work with.

"Maybe she learned it from the TV. Probably some violent movie you let her watch." Yeager was adamantly against the TV for Monkeys program. "What'd you have on this morning? *Scarface*?"

Everyone, including Jan's roommate, Kaci, aggressively faced her.

Jan responded, "Actually, it was *It's A Wonderful Life*. Conga doesn't like violence."

The Institute had access to American Sign Language support: each channel on the TV was accompanied by a person in a circle in the bottom right-hand corner, translating the show into sign language. Sometimes they signed so quickly that even Jan had trouble deciphering what was being said. Conga was content to sit in her beanbag chair and watch classic movies for hours, sometimes signing lines she learned alongside the interpreter. Her favorites included *Carousel* and *Bringing*

*Up Baby*. After this morning's screening, Conga tried signing her favorite line, "I'll give you the moon, Mary," but it came out "I'll give you my dad."

Dr. Walker adjusted his black tie sprinkled with embroidered bananas. "The TV is staying, but we'll have to launch a new publicity campaign. Send this one over to Beth. Get that gorilla a more stable pet. A dog or pig. Something she can't sit on. Something smart enough to know when to hide."


That night, Kaci dragged Jan out to the Lazy Susan on an unwanted double date. Kurt, Kaci's boyfriend, introduced Jan to Andrew, a day trader. He was nice enough, bought her a few rounds of drinks, and coaxed her onto the dance floor, but she felt no spark.

"So how did you get into the monkey business?" Andrew asked when they returned to their vinyl booth. Andrew was sitting too close to Jan, but when she tried to inch away, her exposed skin stuck to the seat.

Jan almost launched into her presentation dialogue, "Well, technically they're not monkeys," but she stopped herself. She wasn't on the clock. After talking with kids and gorillas all day, she had forgotten how to interact with adults.

"My mom was deaf, so signing was like my second language. She had the nicest hands." Jan would sit and watch her mother dance in ballet class. Even though her mom couldn't hear the music, she was able to move with grace across the resin-scented hardwood floors, feeling the vibrations of the piano.

"Man," said Kurt, returning with four more shots of tequila, "if my mom had been deaf I would've played so many awesome tricks on her. Like sneaking up on her and scaring her. You must've done a lot of shit like that."

Jan downed the drink. Her mom had been impressed by anyone willing to use sign language. Jan would have done anything to be able to bring her mom back and introduce her to Conga.

The Lazy Susan was covered in shreds of sawdust, an attempt at charm, but it reminded Jan of a petting zoo. Andrew had been quick to read her mind.

"How often do you think they change this stuff?"

The more tequila they drank, the more Andrew performed the same shtick as every other guy she'd dated. Even his hairy forearm reaching out in front of her to the tray of tequila shots had begun to irritate her. At one point Kurt and Andrew had put their lime wedges into their mouths leaving just the peels sticking out. They raised their arms and made monkey sounds. Kaci was in hysterics. Jan had asked if they could please go home.

Jan was tipsy from the mix of beer and tequila shots.

Up the hill to the IPP staff-housing unit, Jan sat in the passenger seat of the taxi while Kaci and Kurt made out in the back. They weren't supposed to have overnight visitors, but Kaci always broke that rule.

It was drippy out, though not quite raining. A juniper tree whose roots had become too weak to support it had fallen at the intersection of Elm and Fleet and the traffic lights were out. In front of the taxi, two officers wearing white gloves and fluorescent vests were sloppily directing traffic. Jan fixated on their hands as they lazily waved people forward, chatting incessantly. At one point, one of the men even briefly answered his cell phone with one hand, still directing with the other. They finally brought the vehicles coming from the opposite direction to a stop and motioned the cab forward.

It was cheaper living on IPP grounds than paying the high rent in town. The accommodations reminded Jan of her freshman dorm, cramped and smelly, but convenient. A faded pink stucco building offered two-bedroom suites with a kitchenette and a bathroom. Jan had no say about whom she lived with. Institute policy. If primates could be put in an enclosure together and make it work, then so could humans. The only person who found his way out of this was Yeager, who managed to snag a suite all to himself. Some thought it was because he had worked at IPP for so long, but there were stories circulating about fights that ended in threats and resignations.

The cab slammed to a sudden stop and Kaci undraped herself from Kurt. "Aren't you coming up?" she asked Jan.

"Yeah, I'll be right there. I just wanna check on Conga."

"You and that *animal*." Kaci put her arms back around her boyfriend and entered the dimly lit building.

Hoots and screeches accompanied Jan on her walk to the animal habitats. She found the sounds comforting as she walked past the spider and gibbon monkeys, past the howlers and chimpanzees. She stopped to look at her old friends, the orangutans. There were three nylon clotheslines running the length of the enclosure with various items pinned to the lines: a long-sleeved shirt, a pair of jeans, and various socks. Dr. Walker had lauded Jan for her launching of the Monkey See, Monkey Do program, whereby all five of the orangutans had been successfully taught to launder clothing. Luis's hair sat on his head like a disheveled mop, a fallen patriarch. Jan watched by moonlight as Luis scratched his bottom and brought his finger to his nose and nodded, seemingly satisfied that the scent matched his anticipation of it.

At Conga's enclosure, the lights were out. It was Yeager's job to shut them off at eleven each night. Luckily, the moon was bright and Jan could spot Conga in the outdoor area, sitting in a nest of leaves she had assembled, eating fresh stems by sliding her tongue over and around and then chewing them with her back molars. Jan fumbled for her keys, usually attached to her belt loop by a carabiner, but tonight she found them at the bottom of her purse. It felt unprofessional entering the enclosure wearing a skirt, but the tequila gave her courage.

Conga seemed equally grateful to see Jan and rolled over to greet her. She looked like an oversized stuffed animal. Soft purring noises told Jan the gorilla was in a good mood. Her large nostrils flared, hoping to locate some food. She flinched, sensing the alcohol on Jan's breath.

Then she stretched out her long arm and felt for Jan's pockets, still unconvinced that she would have the gall to visit her without bringing a treat.

"No food, sorry." Jan's closed hand for "sorry" looked more like she was putting up her dukes to fight rather than expressing a sloppy apology. The gorilla ignored the signs and continued exploring Jan's front pockets, pulling out a tube of lipstick that Kaci had lent her.

"For my lips." Jan pointed to her mouth. Conga opened the case, smelled it, and shut it. She looked as though she were going to give it back to Jan, but then hurled it into the bushes.

Conga didn't relent and now moved to the back of Jan's skirt, her rubbery index finger hooking the top front of the material. Then she let go and drifted the digit down to its hem.

"Conga, stop it!" But the gorilla continued under the fold of Jan's skirt, in between her thighs and quickly moved her two thick fingers across her cotton underwear.

Jan's leg tingled and goose bumps appeared all over her exposed and now flushed skin. She took a step back from the gorilla.

When Jan regained her composure, she signed, "I go now."

"Goodnight," signed Conga and lumbered back to stick-licking in her nest.

In bed, Jan went over the evening's blurred events in her head. Conga was just looking for food, right? In the oddest of places, no doubt, but looking for food. Gorillas had an exploratory instinct. It was in their nature. In their DNA. But why had it made her feel so good?

The next morning, Jan felt like a dried-out sponge. She hadn't had a hangover this bad since college and threw on a pair of khakis and a white t-shirt with the IPP logo on the sleeve before popping some aspirin.

Kaci's incessant door-banging wasn't helping. "Let's go, hon. You're late. Yeager's threatening to call the boss on you." It wasn't the first time he had made that threat. Jan was someone people usually got along with, which was why Yeager's recent aggressiveness toward her put her on edge.

"Why is he always so nasty to me?" asked Jan.

"Because you're working with gorillas and he's stuck with tree dwellers," said Kaci.

"Pretty," signed Conga when Jan entered the enclosure around ten. She wasn't sure if things would be awkward between the two of them after last night.

"Hug." It was more of a command than a suggestion and Jan listened, knowing very well you don't refuse a three-hundred-pound gorilla.

Jan began a series of mental enrichment exercises. She took a ball out of a storage bin and dribbled it. Conga watched intently.

"You, ball." Jan handed the gorilla the rubber ball. Conga caught on quickly and was soon dribbling it around the inside of her enclosure, navigating around tables and chairs.

"Good!" Jan signed her praise.

After making it past the play stove, Conga began to dribble low to the ground with ferocity. Jan knew to back up out of her way, but she was too late. Conga arched her back, lifted her massive arm and hurled the ball at Jan. It hit her in the head hard, proving that her hangover could indeed grow worse.

"Ouch." Jan pointed to her head and put the tips of her index fingers together, moving them back and forth, the sign for pain. She hoped this would be enough to calm the gorilla. Conga came over like a dog that had peed on the carpet, both begging for forgiveness and attempting to get the ball back.

"Gentle," signed Jan.

Conga seemed to understand. She picked up the ball and held it in her arms, rocking it like a baby. She lovingly stroked it, gave it a sweet kiss, and then lobbed it even harder at Jan, releasing a staccato chortle through her nose. This unpredictability, an unusual display, made Jan nervously think of poor Leg.

The gorilla's patience for mental stimulation was strained so Jan moved on to observation. She stepped back, out of Conga's view, and spent what was left of the morning taking notes. Paperwork used to be tedious, but now she found solace in tracking the recognizable patterns of activity the gorilla exhibited. She recorded Conga's every move on a metal clipboard.

*11:05 stretches arms high. Some mellow barking.*
*11:07 playing with palm frond over head like a wig.*
*11:15 large bowel movement. Northwest corner of habitat.*
Few married couples ever got to be this intimate.

"You shouldn't have been in there with her last night." Yeager confronted Jan while locking up the habitat at the end of the day. She didn't know what to say. What was he doing spying on her anyway? And how much did he see? Jan continued walking.

"She's not your friend, you know. None of them are."

Jan doubted that Yeager had ever had any friends at all, human or otherwise.

Kaci was flipping through a photo album in their living room.

"How was your day?" asked Jan, taking two more aspirin.

"They threw their crap at me again." Kaci was referring to the petulant bush babies she was in charge of. Jan felt so sorry for those animals. They had once been pets but had been seized by animal control services from a man who had kept them locked in a bedroom closet. They interacted, but they didn't understand. However, they did have great aim when it came to throwing their bowel movements at people.

Kaci looked at Jan and started to cry.

"Don't let it get you down," said Jan. "That's what they do! They're just letting you know you're on their turf."

"It's not that. Kurt and I broke up."

"What? When?"

"Today. He said, 'I just can't see myself evolving with you.' What the hell does that even mean?"

Jan shrugged. Who was she to dole out relationship advice?

It means things end without reason, she wanted to say. People change and leave and die and there's no science to it all. But instead, she gave Kaci a squeeze on her shoulder—a sign that things would be okay.

Monday was a long day. Jan had to organize the enclosure for their weekly visitors the next day. After putting away art supplies and picking up Legos, Jan took a seat next to Conga on the oversized trampoline.

"Everyone out there is crazy. You're lucky you're in here," Jan signed.

Conga turned on the TV. End credits were scrolling up the screen. The signer who was usually in the lower left-hand corner was nowhere to be seen; no one could sign fast enough to get all those names in.

Conga seemed to understand Jan's resigned tone and patted her on the head and put her hand up in the air for a high-five. Jan reached up to slap the leathery palm. Conga grasped her hand and squeezed hard. Jan's body was giving her signals—similar to the other night, but this time she was sober. She leaned into Conga's soft chest. Conga reached around and holding her, began swaying in a steady rocking motion, back and forth, like a metronome keeping time for a nocturne. Jan hadn't been held like this in a long time, not since dating her last boyfriend, Ed, over a year ago, and he was a scrawny five-foot seven with a limp grasp and glasses that dug into the top of her head when they hugged.

A gunshot blasted from the television, making Jan jump. It was Casablanca, one of Conga's favorites, but even the opening scene wasn't enough to draw the gorilla away from the coupling.

As Jan was held in a rhythmic embrace that lasted minutes, she had a fleeting moment of panic. She had always been taught to stay in control of any situation with the primates. Being entwined in Conga's arms gave the gorilla all the power. What if she chose to squeeze the life out of her like a boa constrictor? What if Jan couldn't lift her hands in time to sign "stop"? As if Conga had read her mind, she loosened her grip on her trainer. Jan smiled, wiped her eyes, and signed "thanks" to her friend. She felt stupid to have doubted the gorilla.

"More," signed Conga.

"Later."

"Now." Conga reached out to Jan's hips. She pulled her toward her and unclipped Jan's emergency clicker from her belt loop.

"Conga, no." But it was too late; the gorilla had it in her hands and lobbed it on top of the art supply cupboards. Jan would have to call the custodian to get a ladder to reach it. She looked to the gorilla's expressive face to see what she would do next. Jan readied herself for a struggle, her hands in two tight fists clenched to her chest. Conga grabbed Jan's wrist and started grunting, a sign of aggression. Jan looked over to the cupboards to see if there was any way she could somehow scale them to press her clicker, but she was no monkey. Conga jerked Jan toward her and stood up, staring down at her. Jan put her hands up to her face, hoping that whatever Conga was going to do to her would be executed quickly.

"Sit on my face." The gorilla signed quickly so that Jan had to think about it before she realized what she had just said.

"What?"

"Sit on my face." Conga repeated the series of signs.

"Conga!"

"I love you."

"I love you too, but no 'sit on your face.'"

Conga looked disappointed and began nibbling on Jan's right ankle. Jan wanted her to stop, she knew she should stop, but it felt too good. The gorilla's body was warm. She began to tickle and pinch Jan on her arms and legs. Jan reached out to Conga's arm.

"No, like this," she signed, running her fingers over her own forearm, hoping to convey the meaning of a tender touch. Conga then tried moving her hands over Jan's arms and legs. Jan wanted more. She removed her IPP shirt, tossing it onto a pile of Lego pieces. Conga rubbed her hands across Jan's stomach and back. Jan unbuttoned her shorts and let them fall to the floor, giving Conga access to her thighs and buttocks.

The lights went out; Yeager must have been making his rounds.

"Shhh," Jan brought her finger to her lips and Conga obliged, not making a sound until Jan thought they were in the clear. Now, the only light was coming from the TV screen. The voices on the television seemed to whisper:

*Mareichtag and I are speaking nothing but English now.*

*So we should feel at home when we get to America.*

They curled up in a ball on the trampoline, Conga spooning Jan, who folded into her like a chrysalis in a cocoon.

By the time Jan awoke, the lights in Conga's enclosure were back on. Jan was so comfortable resting her head on one of Conga's arms that she didn't want to get up. Had it not been for the pounding she was hearing, she could have slept there forever. She took stock of her body slowly, still naked; she jumped up into a seated position, rousing Conga awake as well.

Her eyes were met by a room full of school kids on the observation deck, mouths agape. Teachers tried to cover their students' eyes and lead them out of the area, to the gift shop, anywhere but here. Conga sat up as well, seemingly unfazed by the visitors.

"Hungry?" Conga held up a palm frond to Jan, who was scrambling to locate her clothing, which was scattered across the enclosure. As she gathered her shorts, shirt, shoes, and underwear from the floor, she looked up again to where her audience had watched her give her gorilla presentation so many times before.

Dr. Walker towered over the clusters of school kids. He must have rushed into the room in the middle of his morning doughnut because his tie was draped over his left shoulder. He gave a knowing nod to Yeager, who appeared to be waiting at full attention. Dr. Walker's eyes locked on Jan and he brought his index finger across his neck in a swift motion.

As the students were shuffled out of the room, a few banged on the glass and a little girl in the corner waved to Jan. Yeager made his way to the entrance of the enclosure and without saying a word, unplugged the TV that was playing a commercial for a boxed set of Cary Grant films. He reached around to hold on to both sides of the flat screen and, bending at the knees, hoisted it up against his chest and took it out of the room. This sent Conga into a fury, pounding her chest, jumping from the trampoline to her art desk to her beanbag.

"Play it, Sam," Conga frantically signed. "You played him, now play with me!"

Jan was reminded of her mother's ballet class, filled with "tongue talkers" as her mom called them. She had often remarked on all the things that non-signers missed out on—the boldness of colors, the beauty of certain movements, and a heightened sense of smell—all muted by the distraction of noise. Her mother would take her place, standing at the barre at the far corner of the studio, wearing a black leotard with a low back, exposing rivulets of sweat that were cradled where the material met in a V, just under her L5 vertebra, the spot where a tail might have protruded had she been a different species.

Words had a definite beginning and an end, but a sign could go on as long as a finger was extended.

# A Real Live Baby

There was an errant magazine, *What the Stork Left*, in Chloe's mailbox when she returned from school on Wednesday, which was weird, too much of a "co-inky-dink" as her friend, Regina, would say, since the ninth-graders had just started their Egg Baby projects. The magazine stood out among the stack of bills and her father's issue of *Smut*, which revealed only hints of body parts behind peek-a-boo paper cutouts. Chloe was always trying to manipulate the plastic wrapping so that she could see behind the strategically placed paper windows, but with little success. The issue of *Smut* would soon disappear into her father's locked bathroom, never to be seen again.

Sitting down on the front steps of her apartment, Chloe began leafing through the pages of the baby magazine, glossy and full of advertisements. They sure made a lot of things for babies: nightlights that twinkled and played music, inflatable bathtubs that fit into regular bathtubs, and little rubber toothbrushes that hug the tip of an index finger like a finger puppet.

Chloe didn't remember anything like that from her own infanthood. Her dad once told her cribs were a waste of money and showed her pictures of how he would just slide the lower drawer of his dresser open and place her in it to sleep.

"It was the perfect size until you turned into a porker."

"Is that a good magazine?" an elderly woman pushing an oversized baby stroller asked.

Chloe quickly closed it. "Not really."

The woman wore tapered khakis and a taupe sweater set. Her hair sat in high-volume fat curls—an unnatural shade of red. "Let me ask you this, whose name is on the back of that magazine?"

Chloe hesitated. "It's mine."

"Bullshit."

Chloe didn't realize old people swore.

"Go on. Pick it up and read the name of the subscriber."

Chloe glanced down at the cover. "Mimi Davies."

"And are you Mimi Davies?"

Chloe shook her head.

"Then that doesn't belong to you, does it? It's a federal offense to steal mail, you know." The woman pulled the magazine away and placed it under her left armpit.

Chloe's cheeks flushed. "How old is your grandchild?" she asked, hoping the question would curb the conversation. She didn't even like babies.

The woman removed the sunshade from the stroller.

"She's my *daughter*. It's amazing what a little in vitro and splash of estrogen can do these days. It's okay. You can look at her. She's sleeping now." The woman pulled the blanket down so Chloe could see her face.

The baby didn't move. Not even a rise of her chest to signal breathing. Her face was too perfect—fair-skinned, blonde ringlets, and lips that slightly parted. The sun reflecting off her cheeks confirmed that she was a plastic doll.

Was Chloe supposed to acknowledge that this baby wasn't real? Should she go along with the charade? Was this some sort of test?

"She's really cute," Chloe said. This would cover her no matter how crazy this lady's intentions were.

"She's six months old. Her name is Winona. And you've probably figured out I'm Mimi Davies. Owner of this magazine," she waved it in the air. "It's an expensive subscription. I like to keep up on the latest gear. Only *the best* for my little girl."

Not exactly the best if they were living on this side of town.

"Ever spend any time with a six-month-old?"

"No." Chloe was hoping to call the old lady's bluff. "She's such a quiet baby."

"Any interest in babysitting tonight?"

To her major disappointment, Chloe had been paired with greasy-haired, nose-the-size-of-Texas, Sid Johnson for the Egg Baby project in Life Science that day. She had hoped to get her crush, Neil Buckman.

Regina had cautioned her in choir that morning. "Jake Florentine was my partner. That's how we started dating. If Shellum likes you, you'll get a good partner."

Mr. Shellum did not like Chloe, at least not if her project partner was any proof. Regina was a senior and Chloe took her advice seriously—like when she suggested Chloe apply toothpaste to her acne and when she told her that if she's ever eating with a guy, she should put the food in her mouth slowly because it's seductive and will make boys like her.

Before Regina could explain exactly what the Egg Baby project entailed, Mrs. Riordan had raised both arms high and then began swinging her hands in four-four time, signaling the sopranos to softly begin their rendition of "Shenandoah."

Choir was the only perfect part of her day. There was order and when everyone followed their part properly, there was beauty.

Chloe had to ace the Egg Baby project. She was failing science and getting Ds or low Cs in the rest of her classes. The only class she really cared about was choir (she had been downgraded to a B+ because she side-talked with Regina) but was recently warned by Mrs. Riordan that she'd have to drop her favorite elective if her academics didn't improve.

She knew her dad wouldn't help motivate her. "I was a straight C student. C stands for 'can do,'" he'd said time and time again when Chloe was feeling down about her lackluster grades.

Mr. Shellum announced in his monotone voice, "Each pair will be assigned a raw egg with my initials on it. You are to share responsibility for this egg for two weeks. If the egg breaks at any time, you fail the assignment. There will be daily check-ins to monitor the well-being of your egg baby."

Chloe was hell-bent on being the best Egg Baby mother in the history of all Egg Baby mothers.

Dinner was Poncho's Tacos. They boasted twenty items that cost less than one dollar. Chloe's dad was still in his green flannel pajamas covered in mooses. Or was it moose? One of those plural words Chloe didn't know how to say. They sat in front of the TV, Chloe on the floor and her dad in his worn lounge chair that had become his permanent resting spot.

"If you got yourself a job, we could have enough money to get one of those chocolate blasters for dessert." Chloe's dad unwrapped a chimichanga from its greasy paper.

"If *you* got a better job, we could eat something other than fast food."

They both started laughing because the truth was, they really loved fast food.

"And besides, I got a job. Starting tonight," Chloe said.

"Yeah right, doing what?"

"Babysitting."

"You? In charge of a baby?"

"What, you don't think I can do it?"

"Babies are hard. Shit. All kids are hard."

"This one seems easy." She didn't tell him it was a doll. She didn't want him to make fun of her or not let her go just because their neighbor was a nut. Better to let him think she had some sort of maternal instinct.

"How much are you getting paid?"

"She didn't say."

Her dad slammed down his Mexican mess. "Always negotiate a price first. That's the number one rule in business. Don't let her ream you up the ass. And make sure your fingers are clean," he added.

"Why?"

"You used to like to suck on my pinkie. All night, pinkie sucking. Wouldn't take no pacifier. My pinkies looked like prunes by the time you were done with them."

"I'll remember that."

He beckoned her close to his face. Chloe leaned toward him, wondering what pearls of wisdom he had to offer her today.

He made a funny gagging sound.

"What the hell was that?"

"I just threw up in my mouth," he blew air in her face.

"That's nasty."

"Don't swear," he pretended to discipline her. "You'll never find a husband. And don't go being a lesbo just to piss me off or I'll write you out of the will."

Chloe knew that all that was being left to her was a worn armchair and seven pairs of flannel pajamas.

The crazy lady opened the door wearing a fancy printed blouse that looked like one of those calyx-patterned Latin vases Chloe was studying in history. A sequined peacock was pinned above her right breast.

"You're late."

Chloe looked down at her watch; late by two measly minutes.

"This is a job, not a luxury cruise," Mimi said. As if Chloe had ever even set foot on a boat.

"Come in and take your shoes off. I like to keep as many street germs as possible away from Winona. You never know what's going around these days."

Chloe took off her ragged green shoes that should have been worn with socks to mask her teen foot funk.

"What's that smell?" asked Mimi.

"Maybe Winona pooped?"

The old lady looked at her and said, "Maybe you're right. You ever changed a diaper before?"

*On a doll, yes. On a real, live baby, no.*

"Oh sure."

"Let's see."

Chloe followed Mimi in to the nursery.

Winona had more toys than Chloe ever had. Her dad's idea of toys included Tupperware containers and empty cans of soda. But this doll had it all: a huge, white crib filled with stuffed animals and a mural made up of hand-painted fairies. Mimi must really love this doll. Next to the comfy-looking rocking chair was a growth chart with photos of Winona.

Some dolls have all the luck.

"What time are you coming home?" asked Chloe.

"You think I'm going to leave a complete stranger with my baby? I'm staying right here to shadow you. You'll just be staying an hour today. Don't worry, you still get paid. Changing table is over there."

Chloe picked Winona out of her bouncer and lay her down on the terrycloth. She lifted up her gingham dress. No flailing legs; this should be easy. She lifted the tabs of the diaper. Did Mimi have to scrutinize her every move? The diaper was heavy with wetness. Chloe had to ignore every urge within to resist sniffing the thing.

"Not too tight!" barked Mimi. "She'll get a rash."

The next fifty-five minutes were spent getting acquainted with the Baby Bible, a thick notebook that held a stack of paper—each in a protective plastic sleeve.

"Tells you everything you need to know about Winona: nap schedules, feeding do's and don'ts, baby CPR, pediatrician information. In fact, I'll give you an extra $2 if you can come up with a piece of information relating to my little one that's not already in there. Always remember to just follow the schedule on page eighteen."

It was an easy $15. Chloe would babysit for real on Saturday.

In Life Science on Thursday, some diligent students showed up with their protective enclosures for their egg babies already completed. Chloe and Sid hadn't even begun. Like couples boarding Noah's Ark, new parents gathered two by two at the front of the class to have their eggs inspected for any damage. Sid had volunteered to take the egg home this week.

"Crack, Ms. Templeton and Mr. Rice. Four points off." Mr. Shellum marked notes in his grade book.

"I see you two haven't completed your housing yet."

Chloe cupped Stella in her two hands. Sid had convinced her it was a strong name that meant "star."

"This part of the project is due on Monday. No way to pass if you don't finish it."

"Want me to come to your house on Saturday night to work on it?" asked Sid.

Chloe wanted to say no. She wanted to tell Mr. Shellum that he had underrepresented single parents, but the science teacher had heard Sid's question and was also waiting for her answer.

"This project can make or break your grade, Ms. Beams. I'd take Mr. Johnson up on his generous offer."

*His generous offer to invite himself over to my house*, she thought.

"Here's my number." Sid grabbed her left hand and wrote wobbly digits on her forearm with Mr. Shellum's Sharpie.

"That will never come off!" said Chloe, looking down at her arm.

"It will enter the pores and be absorbed through the skin in a matter of days, Ms. Beams," said Mr. Shellum. "You'd know that if you'd paid better attention the week we studied the epidermis."

"Did you get lost crossing the street?"

Chloe had arrived at Mimi's three minutes late, this time wearing socks with shoes that she promptly removed.

"I'm rushing out to lunch with the ladies. All the information you need is on a Post-it, stuck to the Baby Bible. I'll call to check in on you two. Make sure you pick up the phone. Once she's asleep, you can watch TV quietly, but bring the video monitor with you. She's been having a hard time with separation lately. She just ate, so be sure you clean up her face. She can be a real messy eater. Well, don't just stand there. Winona is in the nursery in her bouncy chair."

The bouncy chair played an annoying jingle and Chloe couldn't help but sing along in harmony a third above the main melody. Winona couldn't even appreciate her advanced harmonics.

After Mimi left, Chloe consulted the manual. According to page eighteen, bouncy time was officially over.

She went to gather the doll from her room.

"What should we do first?" Chloe grabbed the doll by the foot and carried her into the kitchen, accidentally banging her head into the wooden table.

Mimi hadn't been joking about the baby's cleanliness. There was what looked like dried, caked food on the sides of her mouth, forehead, and hair. It gathered in patches on her pink onesie. Chloe reluctantly sniffed it. Smelled like real food. In the fridge, there were two half-eaten jars of baby sweet potatoes and peas.

The food on the doll's face washed off easily; it was, after all, made of plastic. The baby even had painted veins on her forehead. Why wasn't there anything to snack on in this house besides jars of baby food and fruit cups?

Chloe was tempted to blow off her responsibilities and spend the day watching TV, but then had second thoughts remembering a *Jose Horowitz* show involving a nanny cam that caught the young sitter having sex with her boyfriend on the couch while the kid was busy playing with blocks in his Pack 'n Play.

As she went to put her hair up in a ponytail, the smudged digits on her arm caught her attention. She had yet to call Sid to tell him where she lived.

"Chloe who?" said Sid when she announced herself on the other end of the line.

"From Science."

"Ah yes, fertility goddess."

"How's Stella?"

"She's doing well. She watched me take a shower. I hope I didn't traumatize her too much. What's going on with you?"

"Babysitting."

"Hey, like me."

"Yeah, but I'm talking about a real baby, not an egg." If he only knew how similar their experiences were. "You want my address? I really want to do well on this project." She hoped he heard the urgency in her voice.

"You just really want to hang out with me. Don't deny it."

She gave him her address.

The instant Chloe placed the phone on the receiver, it rang.

"Who have you been talking to?" It was Mimi. "I've been calling and calling and getting nothing but busy signals. This isn't a telethon."

"Sorry."

"Everything okay? Did you clean her up?"

"Yes, she was super messy."

"Did you get her ready for her nap yet?"

"I was just about to get on it."

"The way you kids talk these days. Hand would have been smacked with a ruler in my time."

Chloe stayed silent.

"Well, I'll see you soon. Give my Sugar Bear a kiss for me. Oh and one more thing. On my bed is a small pile of Winona's clothing that needs folding. There are a few of my things thrown in there as well."

Before Chloe could protest, the line was dead.

The "small pile" was more like a mountain. Chloe had gone from babysitter to housekeeper in a matter of seconds.

After shutting off the light in the nursery, Chloe began singing her choral version of "Amazing Grace." She imagined the altos, bases, and tenors singing along with her. She imagined Mrs. Riordan guiding her through *subito forte* and long sustains. Before she even got to the refrain, the neighbor above thumped what could have been a broomstick handle on the floor, ending her lullaby.

This had been the easiest money she'd ever made. She plopped herself on the couch and watched TV until Mimi flew into the apartment.

Mimi flew into the apartment to find Chloe lounging on the couch.

An episode of *Jose Horowitz* was playing. Today was test the baby's DNA and find out who the real father was—and wasn't Molly surprised to find out it wasn't Daniel, the family guy, but Rocco, the one-night stand and professional wrestler. Naturally, a fistfight ensued.

"Well, how is she?"

"Fast asleep."

Chloe held out her hand and Mimi reluctantly placed a twenty-dollar bill in it. Once the money was securely in her back pocket, Chloe added, "I didn't get to all of the laundry."

As she slid her shoes back on and made her way toward the door, Mimi stopped her.

"What are you doing Wednesday? The ladies are coming over for brunch. They're bringing their kids with them. We need a sitter."

There were more of these whack jobs? Or did Mimi's friends have real babies?

"Do I get paid more, being that there are more to watch?" She was turning into quite the businesswoman. Her dad would be proud.

"How about pay and a half?"

"Double pay."

"Fine."

Chloe's dad left a note on the toaster oven saying he'd be out late. Taped to the note was a coupon for Poncho's Tacos.

"Where's Stella?" asked Chloe opening the door for her Egg Baby partner.

"In my cooler," said Sid, rocking the handle of a small lunch box–sized cooler.

"Don't swing her too hard," said Chloe.

Sid unzipped the top of the cooler and there was Stella, nestled in packaging popcorn next to a pack of Ding Dongs.

"Brain food," said Sid.

"What's that on her head?" asked Chloe, looking at the black lines drawn on top of the egg.

"I gave her some hair. Had to give her an identifying attribute. Mom almost put her in an omelet. Some animals do that, you know. Eat their young."

Chloe immediately began worrying about her grade. Mr. Shellum had never talked about the ramifications of adding characteristics to their Egg Babies. She carefully transferred Stella to one of her dad's athletic socks. She put the sock in a fanny pack, leftover from the days when he had collected money as a ferris wheel operator.

"You got any music?" asked Sid.

"I have a CD player in my bedroom."

Once there, they sat on the bed as Sid ate a Ding Dong. She should have taken the time to clean up her room.

"So, how should we make this nursery?"

Sid just shrugged.

"What about that?" The brown plastic packaging of the Ding Dong was perfect. "We could line it with something soft. Cotton balls or tissue."

"What about a lid?" asked Sid.

"We can cut the plastic and then somehow join the two halves together. Protection from all ends."

"No one's laying a hand on my girl." Sid was funnier than she had given him credit for.

"You're going to have to eat the second Ding Dong." He took the chocolate cake out of the packaging and handed it to Chloe, watching as she bit into it. Remembering Regina's advice, she put the food in her mouth slowly and licked her lips. She felt silly. The only person who usually watched her eat was her father. Sometimes, the two of them would have contests to see who could finish their burritos faster. When Chloe finished the last of the snack, Sid passed her a tissue to wipe the cream filling and chocolate off her lips.

"Will you lift your shirt for me?" he asked.

Before thinking whether or not it was a good thing to do, before remembering that she didn't even have a bra on because God had cursed her with a chest as flat as a placemat, Chloe raised her yellow t-shirt.

"May I touch?"

Glancing at the bedroom door to make sure it was closed, Chloe nodded.

They kissed for a while, tongues sloppily exploring each other's mouths, and when he went to take her pants off, she didn't resist. Her dad sometimes had women come over and she would listen to them through the walls. He'd emerge from his room in the morning. "Kid, when your time comes, we'll have a lot to discuss." Regina, just last week in choir, had advised, "Make sure the guy you lose it to is a gentleman."

"Do you want the lights on or off?" Sid's prominent nose thrust into her forehead repeatedly as his body heaved on top of her own. It was all over in less than a minute. Her chin was wet with saliva when they pulled apart. After cleaning herself off in the bathroom, she placed Stella in the sock and the sock in the plastic Ding Dong container, one step closer to acing the project.

"Well, guess we have a plan for the project, so I should go," said Sid. Chloe was relieved to get rid of him. She wanted to think about what had just happened—not spend time with the person it had just happened with.

"I did IT!" she texted Regina, but then immediately regretted it, before placing Stella in the fridge with a "do not eat" sign next to the egg and going to bed.

She awoke earlier than normal the next morning, feeling let down by yesterday's events.

*That's the big deal?* She was sore and spotting a bit, but the Earth had not moved.

"With WHO?" Regina had texted back a dozen times the night before.

But Chloe ignored the texts. She wanted to erase the whole experience. "Revise," like in English class.

Her dad was sitting at the breakfast table with a plastic box in front of him.

"I couldn't sleep well last night. I found this old watch box. Thought it might be good for Stella."

He opened the box. Stella was nestled inside, protected in foam lining.

"Dad! It's perfect!" It was way better than a flimsy Ding Dong container. What were they thinking?

"Thank you!" she said.

"Now you don't have to waste the whole morning on schoolwork," said her dad, eating cereal out of a mixing bowl—a sure indicator that the dishes had piled up in the sink. Chloe had opted for leftover Poncho's. But her burrito wasn't sitting so well with her stomach.

"I won't have time later. I have to babysit."

"That kid again?"

"Yes, the same baby. And some of her friends."

"Hope they're paying you extra."

"Double pay."

"Thatta girl. Next time, Poncho's is on you."

The school day was a blur. Chloe felt like everyone knew her secret. Had Sid told anyone? That kind of information could spread through her school like an STD.

When Chloe saw Regina coming her way, she made a mad dash for the bathroom, where she hid in a stall with her legs up.

She was late to Science and was forced to take the only available seat, next to Sid. Her stomach churned and gurgled. She felt Sid's eyes on her. She watched as his hairy knee angled its way toward her bare leg. When it made contact, she asked to go to the nurse and then left school early.

"WTF?" flashed on her phone multiple times from Regina.

That afternoon Chloe dragged herself over to Mimi's to fulfill her babysitting duties. She should have just canceled.

"Does your dad know you sneak boys into your house when he's not home?" said Mimi.

"What?" asked Chloe, horrified.

"You forget," Mimi said, pointing to her living room window, "I have front-row seats to your escapades."

How much had Mimi seen?

"Plus, you're late again."

An aged woman on the couch holding a black-haired doll offered unsolicited advice. "I always set my watch ten minutes fast. That way I get everywhere I need to be on time."

Next to her sat two more elderly women, one with a bald doll in a sling strapped to her body and the other, giving a rattle to a doll in a car seat.

The circus had come to town.

Chloe removed her shoes.

"Chloe, these are my dear friends, Lacey, Rita, and Shirley."

Chloe waved. The women waved back, the three silent baby dolls did not.

"Where's Winona?" asked Chloe.

"Taking a nap. She'll be up in a minute. She'll need a diaper change when she wakes up. Her daytime schedule is on page fifteen, but you can ask me if you have any questions. The girls and I meet for tea once a month to discuss matters of motherhood."

"Oh! Did you see that new report out about plastics?" said sling mom.

"Yes, got rid of all our plastic bottles on the spot. Replaced them with glass." Rita—or was it Shirley—unstrapped her baby and picked him up out of the car seat. She lowered his raised arm and then glanced at Chloe to see if she had seen.

"Here, you can take him now. His name is Johann. As in Bach."

"I sang 'Gloria in excelsis Deo' in my school choir last year," offered Chloe.

"Yes, you're a real talent," said Mimi. "The upstairs neighbor told me all about it. Maybe you'd like to do a little song for us later?"

Chloe didn't like to sing in front of other people without the security of the choir.

"Maybe," she said, reaching out for Johann. He smelled like vanilla.

"And here's Phoebe. She's gassy—a bit of the colic." Lacey heaved the little one out of the sling.

Chloe rested a doll on each arm.

"And Charlie's a drooler. Must have a tooth coming in. You can let him chew on your finger. It helps relieve the pressure."

Chloe didn't know what to do with the third doll. With an arm wrapped around Johann, she pressed Charlie into her chest and held him with both hands.

"Time for Winona to wake up. You can take them to the nursery so we're not disturbed in here. And don't forget to change her diaper," said Mimi.

Chloe carefully walked out of the room clinging to the three babies. When she reached Winona's room, she dropped them on the floor. They made a soft thud.

"Everything okay in there?" Mimi's voice boomed through a baby monitor.

Chloe found the "talk" button and pressed it.

"Fine."

"Don't forget to change Winnie's diaper."

Did Mimi think she was dense? Just in case one of the "moms" were to walk into the room, she decided to prop up the dolls in various positions. She placed Johann in the Jumperoo, Phoebe on the floor with a small block structure in front of her, and she swapped Charlie for Winona in the crib.

As she removed the cotton onesie, she noted that the diaper did seem kind of bulbous.

She gave it a squeeze. It was full. She eyed baby Winona. She wasn't the kind of doll that had a hole in her mouth where one could put water in it and wait for it to come out the other end. So where had the wetness come from?

She opened the diaper and reluctantly sniffed it. The musty smell of urine jolted her head back and made her eyes wince.

The Mexican food was having a wrestling match with her stomach. "It's like getting traveler's diarrhea without even crossing the border," her father would say when food didn't sit right.

Moving into the bathroom, she pushed and then stalled her sphincter muscles, edging out processed Poncho's into a diaper. She placed the dirty diaper in the Diaper Genie.

*That'll show her.*

Mimi appeared in the doorway.

"These babies need some fresh air. We have a double stroller, a Baby Bjorn, and a carrier. You'll manage. Walk them to the park for an hour."

The park would be filled with neighborhood kids at this time. It was the ultimate humiliation.

"Your ovaries must be so ripe," Lacey said, clutching Chloe's wrist on the way out.

On the walk of shame to the park, she pictured her grape-like ovaries. She didn't get how it all worked inside. At the park, people stared at the girl draped in faux babies. Chloe felt her face redden.

"Can I play with your doll?" a freckle-faced five-year-old asked.

"No," said Chloe.

The girl's mother scowled.

Twenty minutes later Chloe saw Mimi charging toward her, dirty diaper in hand. Chloe left the other three babies in their stroller and carrier. She took Winona out of the Bjorn and scrambled up to the top of the rocket ship slide.

"You think this is funny?" yelled Mimi.

Chloe held onto Winona by the ankle, head-first over the safety railing.

"Leave me alone!" cried Chloe.

Mimi stopped dead in her tracks at the sight of her baby in danger. She screamed and whipped out her cell phone.

The ambulance was followed by two police cars. All arrived in record time. Officers ran toward Chloe, who was now swinging Winona by her ankle.

One officer, upon recognizing the baby as a doll, turned to Mimi.

"Is this some kind of a joke?" the officer asked.

"What?" said Mimi.

"Ma'am, you're under arrest for falsifying an emergency."

"But that's my baby!" She yelled as the officer led her to the squad car. Mimi stared at Chloe from the back of the car.

"Here you go. You can have her." Chloe handed the doll to the freckled five-year-old.

In anguish, Mimi banged on the window from her seat in the police car.

It was finally Friday, the day Chloe would receive her grade for the Egg Baby project. Sid had moved his attention to dour-faced Libby with three cracks in her Egg Baby. For the last time, Chloe held Stella, nestled inside the enclosure of her father's old watch box, and the accompanying workbook pages on the reproductive system for evaluation.

There were flaws in everyone's enclosures: too much ventilation in Carly and Kevin's, allergenic hay-lined flooring in Amanda and Trey's.

"We don't need to talk about it," Sid said when he finally joined her in line to receive their grade. Chloe smiled from ear to ear. Mr. Shellum walked up and down the classroom doling out grades.

Sid and Chloe reached the front of the line.

"Very impressive. An A for both of you."

Sid and Chloe awkwardly high-fived. It would be the last time she'd have skin-to-skin contact with him.

In choir that afternoon, she sat away from Regina and landed a solo. Not the main one—that was given to Aria Adler—but she did get one line in "Shenandoah," all to herself.

Ms. Riordan raised her arms and signaled the beginning of the song, which swooned and heaved through swells and syrupy harmonies.

At that moment she felt as though the world was in perfect pitch, her body working without having to think as an unfertilized egg disintegrated at full presto and was welcomed back by her uterine lining.

# H$_2$O

---

Dear Sward Society and Tennis Club,

As your Association president I am writing to urge you to think with your pockets this holiday season. This is the time of year it is so important to be generous. There's no better way to give back to those who deserve it most.

We are, after all, the Sward Society, our emblem a verdant square of grass. The same patch of grass that greeted our parents and their parents' parents and for the esteemed few like myself and Mr. Henderson, our great-great grandparents. But where's the greenery now, you ask? Sure, water is scarce, but that doesn't mean we should all suffer, right? If those people aboard the Titanic had gone back for those who needed saving, you think anyone would have survived? The answer is no. They would have overloaded the boats. Other people's pain is awful. Let's take a moment to reflect.

But it certainly doesn't mean we should endure having to look out on our grounds here and be met with barren piles of dirt!

So I urge you, during this season of giving, to donate as much as you can (we're aiming for 10 percent of your annual income. That means you, Henderson Family! I know how much Mr. Henderson makes!)

But seriously, people. With everything we've worked so hard for, what's the point if we can't gaze out on beauty? As a wise man once said, "A thing of *beauty is a joy forever." Our goal is to green the sward, but if we can raise beyond that, the landscaping possibilities are endless. Even with the water restrictions.*

*Thank you so much for your understanding.*

*Our future members of the Sward Society will be so grateful you didn't let them down.*

*Sincerely,*

*Bunny Newton*

*P.S. We're getting the very first shipment of proprietary H$_2$O in two weeks for sale in the tennis shop (thank you once again, Mr. Henderson!)*

### Day 1

I was rooting around old boxes, searching for moist wipes (We're out. How the children are supposed to bathe is beyond me.) when I came across this journal. A blank notebook is so full of hope and promise. Plus, perpetual dehydration makes me forgetful, so perhaps it's a good idea to use it for documentation. I read that writing your feelings down can be cathartic. If that's the case, everyone should have a journal—unhappiness is an epidemic.

It's supposed to be getting even hotter this week. There are red flag alerts all over the TV and radio stations.

Because they're under eighteen, the kids get government-subsidized water delivered every morning. It's the lowest quality. And full of bleach. But it keeps them hydrated. Keeps their little bodies moving. I have to buy my own at the Cent and Dime down the street. They sell it in an opaque container, which is probably a good thing because I feel things floating in the water. I don't wish to investigate further. I've done some mathematical calculations and I've decided that every tenth quart I purchase gives me some sort of stomach bacteria. At least the kids don't have that problem. But when it's sweltering like this, they want more and I have no way of giving it to them. We have to ration.

## Day 5

My latest aim is to steal one bottle of water a day from the ladies at the Sward Society. They're swimming in the stuff. So far, I've had about a 40 percent success rate. When I come home the first things the kids do is turn their heads away from the TV and ask, "Good water?" If I say, "yes," they hoist themselves off of the bedbug-ridden couch (it's a misnomer those bugs limit themselves to beds) and lumber over to me in a zombie-like fashion, arms extended. If I fail to procure the water, their glazed eyes return to the illuminated screen.

The kids don't go to school anymore. The walk there was making them use up too much energy. Even people who can afford enough water don't send their kids to school. The women at the tennis club all have private tutors who come to them. (Why do they even call it a tennis club? No one plays. It's too dehydrating.) But Rex and Anna are home full-time now. They mostly watch TV, even though it's practically all commercials these days. They like the commercials. Rex says when he grows up he wants to be a commercial producer. "I'll get anyone to buy anything." Get someone to *buy us a new life*, I want to tell him.

I walk slowly from home to the club. I'd rather be docked pay for being late than move too quickly and be forced to drink too much water. I used to love potato chips, but now I'm salt-free. It keeps the thirst down. The walk is brown. All shades. Mud. Tan. Beaver. Ecru. Sepia. Burnt umber. Russet. There was a push a while back to have everything be California Native, but even the native plants were like, "Are you kidding me, folks? We need water once in a while!" In my head the plants talked like Jimmy Durante. Then they all died.

I miss green things.

Tree falling is a problem in a big city like this. They dry up at the roots and without any warning, a decaying tree will just land on you, like a guillotine coming down. I've lost a few friends that way. I avoid the streets with the trees now.

The Sward Society sits at the top of a hill, behind iron gates. I have to show my ID badge at the bottom before making the trek up. Slowly. Sometimes I walk backwards. I try not to think about water. Ice-cold water with ice cubes that clink in the glass. It's a sound I have to endure all day at the club. It sticks in my head like a song I can't shake. I pretend the women are drinking vomit.

"What's that smirk across her face?" Bunny Newton says loudly so I can hear. She and Alice Henderson and a few other regulars practically camp out there every day. I have to wait on them. Mist them. Adjust the fans.

The next time I serve Bunny I replace her glass with my water from the Cent and Dime. The past nine bottles have been intestinal-upset-free. Maybe it will be her lucky day. I hand her the glass of water in a dark tumbler, so she can't see the mysterious floating particles, and watch as she downs the whole thing in front of me as though she were trying to wave her thirst-quenching prowess in my face.

I cleaned the bathrooms myself this morning so I know they'll be to her liking when she has to spend the rest of the day there until the SUV with the blackened windows comes to take her home. If they can't see outside, they don't have to think about our suffering.

*Memo to: Liquid Nation Branding Department*
*From: Derek Henderson, CEO, Liquid Nation*

*In the past, Liquid Nation water products have been marketed as sturdy, reliable, nurturing. With the launch of our new upscale brand, $H_2O$, we're taking hydration to a whole new level. But $H_2O$ is a different kind of brand. You may be wondering why we're even bothering to advertise when only 1 percent of the population can afford $H_2O$, but surveys have shown that by exposing the rest of the population to what they don't have, not only do we boost the value of $H_2O$ but our marketing research has shown that sales soar with our other brands! (SOAK and DRENCH, to name a few.)*

*Don't believe me? Ruminate on the rhinoceros. You think people want* them running around, bucking and impaling other animals and people? But when a hunter shoots one and it dies on the spot and that hunter skins and beheads it and preserves it on a wall . . . when that hunter pays upwards of $1 million for the chance to kill a black rhino . . . he thereby increases the value of the rhino exponentially. People running in the plains feel closer to greatness.

It's the same with water, which is why we're going for sexy with this product. This is what I want in our debut commercial and I want it fast. Picture a parched woman on a deserted island. This woman is our ideal consumer— fringed suede two-piece bikini. Marooned yacht floating in the background. She steps over her dead butler, who's on the beach being eaten by crabs.

The woman is crawling like a child, but you know, more like a sexy baby across the sand moving toward something. Her mouth remains open in the shape of an O. She looks beautiful. But desperate. She sees something golden in the distance.

She moves toward it. It's a bottle of H2O. She's almost too weak to open it (but it's the new snap top, so it's a cinch). She takes a small sip of water. The camera turns away to the setting sun. When it pans back, she's returned to her full beauty. Hair done. Sarong on, fabric trailing in the wind. She looks at the camera and says, "H2O" but the "O" is more of a groan. A prelude to an orgasm.

A small asterisk states at the bottom of the commercial:

*$199.99 delivery guaranteed within ten minutes of order being placed.

Let's get this up and running in the next few weeks.

## Day 10

I can't stand my own children's smell anymore. What put me over the edge was that jingle for dry soap:

"You don't have to get wet to get clean."

It's lodged in all our heads. But the kids know better than to ask for it. We can only spend money on food.

"Bath time," I announce. Anna's eyes light up.

"You got some dry soap!" she says.

"I got this instead," I say, sticking my tongue out at her. They undress and like a mother cat, I lick a cloth until it is saturated and wipe them both down. Licking and wiping. Licking and wiping until there are no more dirt marks or crusts in creases.

"We don't smell better," says Rex.

I crush some dried rosemary in my hand—it had been part of a holiday wreath so many years ago—and rub the leaves up and down their bodies. Rex dry-heaves. Anna smells herself.

"That's better, Mommy," and she kisses the top of my head. Oh to be five and sweet.

*Dear Sward Society and Tennis Club,*

*Welcome to 2055! Another great year ahead here in our little slice of heaven!*

*You may have noticed some changes have taken place! Are you feeling green with envy! We sure know nonmembers are every time they pass by and see the most realistic collection of fake botanicals west of the Mississippi!*

*We have one more teensy-weensy favor to ask of you (We know you won't let us down) but before that, we wanted to assure you that just because the government says we have no right to fill our pools with water, we think differently. Sure, the outdoor pool can be detected by drone, so for now, your little munchkins can practice their skateboarding (helmets and other protective gear are available for rent in the gift shop) and if you have any other ideas for the empty outdoor pool, please feel free to pass them along. And no, Mr. Henderson, naked wrestling is not on the approved list of activities (just kidding, Alice! wink wink!)*

*So, this is the part where I have to ask for something. But I know you'll see the value. First I want you to think back to what it felt like to stroll through your own rose garden. Remember? You'd meander, wave to the gardener, perhaps cut a few stems for an arrangement in the living room (Alice, remember the arranging party we had? Mr. Henderson reached his arm around me thinking I was you, but instead was met with my pregnant belly!)*

*Remember the smell of those roses? Delphina's even served that rose ice cream! It paired perfectly with champagne! Anyhow, what I'm trying to do in evoking all these wonderful memories is not depress you (yes, ladies, our asses were higher and yes, men, your six packs weren't covered in layers of blubber) but we want to bring some of those smells back! I have found an amazing small business that will come and—get this—apply any fragrance of your choice to the artificial flora. Want these green leaves to smell like Louise Odier, Fragrant Plum, or Just Joey? Consider it done!*

*The company is in Paris and can ship their product in a climate-controlled cooler overnight for the cool price of $4,000. We can do this, people. What's that you say? You can't? Oh, skip your Botox injections for one week, Alice! Learn sacrifice, people! For the greater good of our amazing community! We're showing people how it's done!*

*à bientôt!*
*Bunny Newton*

## Day 14

"Good water?" Rex and Anna ask when I come home.

I nod *yes* while they're still asking the questions. They come to me weakly. Articulated bones through worn shirts.

They take turns guzzling to their heart's delight.

"Not too quickly," I warn them and they slow their frantic drinking.

Today's water is courtesy of Bunny Newton, who quickly tossed the bottle aside when Alice Henderson came to the club touting her husband's latest and greatest water product, $H_2O$.

"It hasn't even been released to the public yet. Derek is working on the commercial," as if water needed any advertising to make people want it.

Bunny punted her bottle of water like a football and it landed under a dying pepper tree. When the ladies left, I went over and scooped it up before Raoul, the groundskeeper, could spot me. Technically, the bottle was supposed to go to lost and found.

Rex and Anna take a post-rehydration nap. When they resume their

TV watching, it's back-to-back commercials. Polls show it's the most-watched hour.

*Buy your dew catch-all today!*

*Lye doesn't lie—for all your outdoor toilet hole needs.*

*Try Bird Jerky! You catch 'em, we cure 'em. Let us be the jerk!*

The sun has dipped and I open a can of dehydrated corn beef. It slides out in perfect cylindrical form. I slice it three ways.

Dinner is served.

## Day 18

Before they could rip out all the Sward Society's old plants and throw them away, I snapped a nub off one and put it in my pocket. In the wild, this particular plant grows fleshy, snakelike leaves and when they flower, the petals are white. The piece I took is pale green. No leaves.

Raoul caught me. "*Dudleya edulis*. Nice choice."

"What?" I asked.

"That's the Latin name. Most people just called it Fingertip. You'll never be able to keep it alive. Do you know what's in the government water?"

I had heard rumors. Hormones, medicine, sewage water. But if it keeps me alive, surely it could keep this plant alive. Plus, I want my kids to touch a real thing.

"Good water?" Rex and Anna ask.

"A plant," I say.

They are delighted by my gift.

"Let's name it," says Anna.

"That's stupid," says Rex.

"You're stupid," says Anna. "Let's call it Al."

Rex pulls down his pants, "Hey Al, want to see my butt?"

"Don't!" Anna shrieks at a decibel that reaches deep in my ear canals.

"You're not gonna give that thing any of *our* water, are you?" asks Rex.

We've all become guardians.

I calm his fears. "Of course not. I'll share mine. It doesn't need very much."

*Memo to: Liquid Nation Branding Department*

*Kudos to everyone in marketing. Our commercial nabbed the number one spot. Sales are through the roof. Fun fact: police have arrested a ring of criminals slapping fake $H_2O$ water labels on that disgusting government-subsidized water. But all this buzz is good for our brand.*

*I'm thinking it's time we up the ante. Sure, our commercials are sexy. But since FCC regulators are no longer doing their job, I say we push it. Forget about being sexy. I think this water should make people want to fuck. You know what I mean? Isn't that what you want to do when you feel hydrated? When you feel at the top of your game?*

*So get this. Attractive couple. It starts to rain. We'll have to use blue screen. Our whole operation will get shut down if we use real water for a rain scene. Dead bodies cover the ground. it starts to rain and it's a miracle because, well, it hasn't rained in . . . 550 days. Our man and woman rise with hope in their eyes. They lick the rain. Seductively. They notice each other. They're soaking wet now (clad in white, of course) But the rain isn't enough to quench their thirst. A light beams down on a dirt patch and the couple starts digging. They've found buried treasure. They unearth it and inside is $H_2O$. This is where it gets good. They pound it and once they're done, they have stamina. They have sex drive. Then they just go at it. (I'm telling you NO one is working on FCC shit these days . . . remember when the toilet paper company showed that commercial of the guy actually taking a dump? Everyone's too weak to fight. This will go through.) The man and woman climax together. The voiceover says "$H_2$" and she finished with an "Oh!!!!" And scene.*

*Find two attractive people from the shelter who are willing to have sex on camera. Make sure they can get it on one take because we don't want to waste the drinking water on them. One bottle each. That's it.*

**Day 25**

"Al's changing colors," says Anna.

It was true. It had only been a week and he was already browning. How can I keep children alive if I can't even keep a four-inch plant alive? Do my kids really need to experience death anymore than they already have?

"Al's dying," says Rex, causing Anna to cry.

"Don't cry!" I warn. "Remember what happens to your water levels when you cry. Anna, please stop." I scare her quiet. And then turn on the TV.

But she doesn't want to watch.

"He needs nice words," says Anna. She takes the plant from its perch on the counter and places it on the floor. Lying on her belly, she puts her face close to Al.

"We love you, Al. You're my very best friend." She pets his drying leaves.

I stroke Anna's thinning hair. "He'll be fine. I promise."

A mother should never make such promises.

*Dear Sward Society and Tennis Club,*

*I'm going to skip the formalities and get straight to the point. Someone is stealing our fake plants. I know. It's shocking that in this sort of tight-knit community—among the pillars of society, we'd have a thief among us.*

*Perhaps my conjuring those fond memories in the rose garden was too much for one of you? Well, to you I say, we still have therapists! You don't even have to leave the comforts of your home—they'll see you over the computer. To you I say, how do you sleep at night? Every time you walk by a stolen plant, I know pangs of guilt haunt you. To you I say, what about the children?*

*That is all.*

*No wait, that is not all.*

*I am here to announce our game plan. I'm just going to lay it all out on the table. When have I ever been one to make poop smell like roses? (Sorry to bring up the roses again.) We need $50,000 for security cameras. We will need* *to take rotational shifts watching the recorded tapes so we can catch this hooligan among us—this wolf in sheep's clothing. I'm hoping that the threat of the cameras will be enough to deter you—yes, I'm talking to YOU from ever trying this again.*

*Thank you,*
*Bunny Newton*

*P.S. You may have noticed we are understaffed these days. For most, the commute to work is achievable only by foot, which apparently has sent a few of our best to the ER or worse. (gulp!)*

*It's like my mother once said when I gathered up all the snails I could find in the garden (they were eating mother's roses) and placed them in a terrarium in my room. I'd watch them create sticky trails for hours. What was it Mother said? Ah yes, "Don't get attached."*

## Day 26

My throat is like a desert after work. It was the longest walk home I've ever taken. I'll get right to the point. I was fired. I was supposed to be spraying the women with the mister and I did a fine job. I worked hard to time my sprays perfectly, pressing the button only when the women weren't talking. They don't like it in their mouths. Just on their faces, like an ocean spray. I thought they were all turned in the other direction to breathe in the vanilla fragrance they had chosen for their new fake plants when, without thinking, I sprayed myself. It was the most pleasure I've felt in years. Alice Henderson saw and called me out. I had nothing to say. She told Bunny, who fired me on the spot. But I didn't go softly into that cold night. I told Alice the truth—all about how Bunny Newton has been screwing Mr. Henderson. I told her how I caught them on the Sward. I had video proof. (It happened before the cameras were stolen. I watched the tapes when I got bored.) As I left, they were engaged in a full-on fistfight. They broke golden rule number four at the club, **NO FUCKING ON THE SWARD.** Well, that's not really the rule. The rule is more like,

"Members shall act as upstanding citizens at all times. Violation of this rule may result in immediate expulsion."

So I can only assume they'll be tossed out too. Then we'll have something in common. This place won't be around much longer anyway. They're down too many employees.

During their melee, I took it upon myself to steal a golden bottle of $H_2O$ and hide it under my t-shirt and then transfer it to my backpack on my way out.

It was another ninety-eight-degree day in December. I got to thinking about topography on the way home. When the cracked sidewalk elevated even an inch or two, it felt like I was climbing Mount Everest. My calves begged me to stop, but my thirst kept me going. I just had to get home and show the kids the $H_2O$ I had stolen.

More and more bodies scattered the streets. They can't clean them up fast enough. There's nothing more to do but step over them. Step around them. If anyone knew what I had in my bag, I could have been killed. Over a bottle of water.

"Good water?" I wait for them to ask.

"Gold water," I respond.

I show them the bottle.

"Just like on the TV!"

"It's a fake!" Rex said. He'd seen the reports on the news.

"I promise. It's not," I said. "See? The label doesn't peel off because it's etched into the bottle."

He tried to peel off the label and realized that I was telling the truth.

Their eyes widened, dislodging some crust on Anna's left eye, which she picked at with her fingernail.

How they used to love their baths.

"Sip?" she says. I nod and helped her. The bottle is heavy for her frail body.

Rex tries some afterwards.

"It tastes perfect," he says. "Let's save it for after dinner."

"Golden dessert," says Anna, licking her lips.

I place the water on the counter.

I want it too, but I need to change out of my bloody clothing and tend to my blisters, which are caking and red.

Tomorrow I will wake up and have nowhere to be. Tomorrow we can all stay in bed and watch TV together. When my feet are taped and tucked in a pair of breathable socks, I head downstairs. I moisten the space between my teeth and my lips in anticipation of the $H_2O$. It is a small, temporary fix, but I know this sip will bring me hope. Rex is lying on the couch watching TV. The bottle is gone.

A woman on the TV rises from the dead in the rain.

"Where's the water?" I ask Rex, panicked.

A wet woman and a wet man find each other among a sea of dead bodies.

Rex shrugs his shoulders.

Moving to the kitchen as fast as I can, I find Anna sitting on the floor observing Al, who is drowning in a pool of water.

"What have you done?" I yell.

"Al was very thirsty. Al was going to die. So I gave him a drink. Then I spilled it."

Rex pushes past me and begins lapping up the water off the floor. Not a lot of water is going in his mouth because it's dispersed across the ground. But his tongue is doing an efficient job of cleaning the floor.

The TV blares what sounded like porn.

I am too tired to move. I am too tired to yell. I am too tired to care. And I have a pounding headache.

I stay on the floor with Anna, trying to hold back salty tears.

# Stuffed

———

You cannot play chess if you are kindhearted.

—*French proverb*

In total, there were seven mounted heads at the Makin' Bacon Café. Three deer (two does, one buck), a fox, a chipmunk, a rabbit, and a black bear hovered over the tables of tourists like spies—as though at any moment they might start speaking to each other or drool onto the plates of burnt hash and soggy oatmeal below.

Most people took little notice of them. What was a dead animal hanging from a wall when there was a dead animal on a plate? Now *that* was something!

But the boy noticed the hanging heads the first time his parents dragged him, by his bony shoulder, into the joint. By his third visit, he was desperately determined to sit under the fox. Foxes were clever. The boy's father, oblivious of the gigantic head, took a seat, once again, under the bear.

The threesome ordered their food and looked through yesterday's vacation photographs: the fishing store with its array of shiny tackle and feather rigs and then the candids taken at the bustling mall. The boy had enjoyed the food court the best.

"Can I sit over there?" the boy asked the wiry waitress, pointing to the empty booth under the fox, when she brought him his bowl of hard-boiled eggs.

His parents dug into their corned beef hash topped with two eggs over medium.

The waitress leaned in close to the boy and smiled wide. She was missing her left canine tooth.

"You have a seat anywhere you'd like, honey."

The boy looked to his parents for approval.

"I don't care for this," his mother said, shoving the half-eaten plate of food toward the waitress. "I'll try the Endless Plate of Pancakes instead."

"We're gonna be here a while," said the boy's father. "Go on." He brought his hand up in a shooing motion as though he were swatting a fly. The boy understood the signal, grabbed his chessboard, slingshot, and bowl of hard-boiled eggs and moved to the empty table under the fox. Once seated, he gnawed at an egg, taking care not to let any of the yolk make its way into his mouth.

"The usual, Nora?" asked the waitress.

Nora nodded. She began every morning with a cup of coffee in town. She could have just as easily made it at home, but her time at the diner would be the only human interaction she'd get all day.

"He likes your heads," said the waitress, handing Nora the hot mug.

Nora watched the boy admire her handiwork. He probably thought the fox's eyes were real. He probably assumed the fox's brain was still tucked cozily inside its head.

The boy stared up at the animal, taking stock of its auburn and white fur. Its teeth were exposed in a snarl and he wondered if it was growling at whomever it was that killed him. He wanted to touch the pelt, but he couldn't reach his hands high enough. He wished the fox would magically come to life and play chess with him. The boy was tired of playing by himself because he always won. Likewise, he always lost. Each and every time.

The boy set up the black and white pieces just as they had been this morning before he had to stop abruptly to get in the car. White had captured two pawns. Black, a pawn and a bishop. The boy zipped up his hoodie all the way, concealing his "Shop till you drop" shirt, a freebie with purchase during yesterday's outing.

"Hard to play a decoy when you're playing yourself," a meaty woman in a flannel button-down said.

The boy looked at her.

"Want a real opponent?" she asked.

"You play?" he said, putting the egg back in the bowl and then smelling his fingers to confirm that they did indeed smell like egg.

"It's been a while," she said, taking a seat across from him.

The boy looked over at his parents, wanting to make sure it was okay that this stranger sat down with him, but they had their faces buried in their breakfast. He hoped some sort of protective parental instinct would kick in if this woman was, in fact, dangerous.

"Skittles," he said.

"The candy?"

"No, it means a casual game of chess. No clocks."

"Oh, yes. Skittles. You set up your side first and I'll follow."

The boy arranged his black pieces in record time, then helped the woman with hers. He badly wanted to be playing against the fox instead of this woman.

"You go first," she said.

He moved his pawn and she did the same. After five turns the boy had taken her knight and queen. *Woodpusher*, he thought. He wondered, if he had said that out loud, whether she would even recognize it as an insult. He could have beaten her right away, she was such a weak player, but instead, he wanted the game to last as long as possible. No one ever played chess with him.

"You're forcing me to try and solve a problem I don't want to have," his father would say.

At least now the boy got to try out a bunch of moves he had been studying: Alekhine's Gun and the mysterious rock move, which she obviously fell for.

When he couldn't prolong the game any further, he went in for the kill. This was his favorite part.

"Checkmate," he said.


Nora feigned being stabbed in the chest. She held her hand over her heart and fell backwards across the booth. She made more noise than she had meant to and the waitress came running over.

"Are you all right, Nora? Should I call an ambulance?"

"Sorry. I'm fine," she said, removing her hands from her chest.

The waitress gave Nora that look she often received, falling somewhere between pity and annoyance.

The boy looked up at the fox.

"You like him?" Nora asked.

The boy nodded.

"I named him Eddie after a boy I used to have a crush on."

The boy looked over at his parents, who waved back encouragingly.

"I name all the animals I stuff," she said.

"What do you mean, stuff?"

"Well, they don't just freeze in time on their own. There's a whole science to it. I never kill any animals; they all make their way to me. Some roadkill, others through hunt, some I just happen to find at the end of their lives and I preserve them, so they can live on."

"But how do you do it?"

"It's a whole process. Complicated. Like chess."

"Can I see?"

No one had ever asked to see Nora's workshop. Sure, they all were kind to her when she offered her practice heads to the diner, but it was more in a "Oh, that's quaint, Nora" kind of way. Other people did pay for her work, sometimes. But no one in town took her seriously.

The boy's parents finished their meal and headed toward their son.

"You found someone to suffer through that game with you," the boy's mother cackled. He hated it when she cackled.

"This is Nora. She stuffs the animals," said the boy.

"Animals?" asked his mother.

"The ones all around here," said the boy, motioning to the seven heads affixed to the diner's walls.

"We have to get going. Tina's Tinies opens at ten o'clock sharp!" said his mother.

"Can I see how she does it?" asked the boy.

"Does what?"

"The animals."

His mother shifted her purse to her other hip, revealing the salt and pepper shakers she had pilfered from the table. "Chops off their heads and dips them in varnish, I suppose. Now let's go!"

"Please, Mom."

The mother looked at Nora. They had a similar build.

The waitress passed by with an Endless Plate of Sausage and paused, overhearing their conversation. "Nora's practically a preschool teacher. So good with kids. I'd even trust her with my three cats. I can't say that about most people."

"You babysit?" asked the boy's mother, turning to Nora.

The boy hated that word. He was nine years post-baby.

"It's been a while, but I suppose . . ."

"It would be nice for us to get a break just for a few hours. We've been cooped up together in that camper for so long." She looked at Nora. "You don't mind taking him." It was more of a statement than a question. "We can meet you back here at three."

As soon as Nora had agreed to the arrangement, she was nervous about being responsible for something living; she was used to caring for the dead. At least it wasn't far to Nora's home. They turned off the main road and took a left at the fork that led to a dirt road that went up, up, up.

"My legs hurt," the boy said. "And this is digging into my skin." He removed the slingshot from his back pocket and held it up.

"Almost there," said Nora. She had no idea how long a child could walk before tiring out.


The cabin sat isolated at the top of the road, surrounded by trees. There was a large porch, and a towering pile of wood formed a pyramid to the right of the front door.

"Come in. That's my bedroom and a kitchen to the right, but to the left is where I do my work."

They entered the house and were greeted by an iron beast of a stove. And more piles of wood.

"That's my heater, for the winter," Nora explained. "When the snow comes, that wood there keeps me alive."

The boy wondered about all the things that kept him alive. Wood wasn't one of them.

The rumble of a fridge motor greeted them as they paused at the door to her workspace. Nora flipped on the lights. It smelled like chemicals and trash. The boy held his nose.

"That's the maceration. It's one of the worst smells in taxidermy. That's a walk-in refrigerator where I keep the animals until they're ready to come out and play. They were convinced I was a survivalist when I had them install it. They're right, I guess, in a way. I mean, everyone needs a job to survive!" She patted the boy on the back a little too hard and he stumbled forward.

He followed her past the fridge to a large room with a huge table taking up most of the space. The walls were lined with shelves populated by tools and cans and gloves, haphazardly placed.

"I get sent animals from all over. Mostly from museums and zoos, but sometimes by individuals, usually hunters. These are all the tools I use."

The boy looked at the tool collection in wonder. This was more fun than Monday's visit to the candy shop had been. His parents had purchased extra-large jawbreakers. But he preferred the small ones. He could fit the whole thing in his mouth.

"You've got your gimlets, wires, and bone cutters over here. And here are the brushes. Not for your hair." She grabbed a brush and brought it to her own head of hair without making contact.

"You're like a surgeon!"

"No, I'm not healing anyone," said Nora. "And here are the scalpels and knives."

The boy's eyes widened.

"Here's what I've been working on," Nora held up the woodchuck. "I named him Chuck. Not too clever of me. Want to name him something else? Anything you want."

"Chuck is fine," said the boy.

"I had to extract the muscles and brain. I used wire to put him in a nice pose. Some people like to position them as though they were cartoon characters." She hated the kitsch assignments. Just last week she'd had to set up a squirrel wedding. The rodent bride held a bouquet of baby's breath. Nora couldn't afford to be too picky, but the boy didn't have to know that. He could think she had integrity. She tossed some lace she hadn't cleared up onto the floor so the boy wouldn't see.

"That's what you want in the end," Nora said, "to recreate the jizz."

"The jizz?"

"The stuff that makes them look their most natural. I want to bring out the best in these animals so I construct an illusion. Sometimes the end result is better than the original. Here, want to varnish Chuck's nose?"

She handed the boy a paintbrush and motioned for him to dip it in the can.

"What does this do?" he asked.

"Makes the nose look wet. Makes it more real."


The boy took the brush and dipped. It was like painting in art class. He hated art class, but he liked this. This felt important. He brought the brush to the tip of the woodchuck's nose and blotted.

"That's good! Why you're a natural!"

The boy smiled and admired the stiff animal, now with a wet nose. She was right. Chuck did look more alive.

Nora showed him some other animals, all in various stages of preservation: two raccoons, an owl, a family of ducks.

"I'm weaving a nest for this scene. I find nest building difficult with ten fingers. I don't know how these birds do it with only a beak." She put her hands behind her back and picked up a twig in her mouth and tried to place it on the half-built nest. The boy smiled and did the same. He giggled as he flapped his faux wings and awkwardly placed more sprigs on the nest. He had never tried being a duck before.

"Want to remove a brain?" Nora asked. The boy eagerly nodded.

By the end of the afternoon the boy had thawed a hawk, filed artificial claws on a rabbit, and de-brained a robin.

"You're very dexterous," Nora complimented. "You lose it with age, you know."

The boy stared at the brain in the bowl in front of him.

"It's shaped like an egg," he said.

"That's the optic lobe," said Nora. The boy didn't know what that meant, but he nodded as though he did.

When it was time to go home, Nora didn't make the boy clean up anything. She led him out the door, out of the woods, and back to the diner, where his parents were sitting in the same bear booth, unwrapping their miniatures.

"He's alive!" joked his father, when he saw the boy and then tousled the top of his head, making the hair stick up sloppily.

"Want a doughnut?" his mother asked.

The boy was excited for this treat, but his enthusiasm waned when she handed him a miniature plastic chocolate-glazed doughnut the size of his pinky fingernail.

"Isn't that the cutest?" His mother and father were now in hysterics looking down on a miniature feast. Nora stood awkwardly by the table. To make the moment disappear, the boy imagined lining up all his parents' miniatures and shooting them, one after another, with his slingshot. He'd been told he was an excellent shot.

"For your troubles," the boy's father said, handing Nora some wadded-up bills.

"Thank you. Smart boy you have. Picks things up quickly," said Nora.

The boy waved good-bye to his favorite fox head, but Nora must have thought the gesture was for her and she vigorously waved back.


That night, Nora sat in her bed with a cup of Earl Grey. She didn't own a TV. She sat drinking her cup of tea and studying the fleur-de-lis on her comforter. Who had come up with that design? And why had it appealed to her?

She stared at an individual fleur-de-lis until it started to shift and lurch⊠the two side figures hunched over as though they were throwing up, bound to the tall middle figure by a tight belt. She had the sudden urge to cut the blanket to pieces.


The boy's parents couldn't be bothered to give him the keys to retrieve the chess board out of the car. There was nothing to pass the time, so he had grabbed the slingshot and gone outside instead.

They wouldn't know if he left the grounds. They were busy watching TV and drinking beer out of mugs shaped like oak trees.

It had taken both hands to steady the bird. At first it tried clumsily to flee and the boy had to grip harder until the bird's feathers became damp from the boy's clammy palms.

The bird's beak was agape. How did such a delicate creature exist? Why couldn't its flesh just bruise like the boy's own flesh? Did the bird's skin look dimpled when naked, like a Thanksgiving turkey?


There was a faint knock at Nora's door.

Who would possibly be up in the woods at this hour? She listened again. And the delicate knock repeated. She imagined deer antlers scraping her front door. It had been ages since an animal had come to visit her. It was as though they could smell the death and decay inside her studio and they steered clear.

She got out of bed and put on her robe before opening the door.


The boy stood there in his pajamas and sweater, zipper open, exposing a chest covered in cotton rocket ships. He lifted his hands, presenting her with a stunned male blue jay, a full crest of feathers on its head.

"Where did you get this?"

"It flew into my window tonight. I thought you could stuff it."

"But it isn't dead."

"I think it will be." The boy regretted not helping the bird die on the way over.

She looked at the bird. It was shivering from shock. Its legs buckled in her palm. It opened and closed its eyes slowly.

"Sometimes they just react to the blow. Sometimes they come out of it and recover."

"Oh," said the boy disappointed.

They stood there observing the bird for quite some time. The bird looked at her and then at him. It began moving rather erratically, trying one last time to spring loose from Nora's fleshy palm before succumbing to death.

Nora wiped away a tear.

"Is it dead?" the boy asked.

Nora nodded.

"Now can we stuff it?"

"Come back tomorrow. I'll have more of a plan."

"But I leave tomorrow!"

"It won't be high quality in one night."

"I don't care. Can we stuff it?" He begged.

Nora's studio was cold. She placed some wood in her furnace and took out the toolbox labeled "small animals." The bird lay limp on the table. Nora could tell its floppy neck made the boy shudder. She examined it from all sides. There was blood on the back of its head.

"You said it flew into a window," Nora sounded angry.

"Yes," said the boy.

"But it has blood on the back of its head like something was thrown at it."

The boy simply shrugged.

Nora placed latex gloves on her hands. The boy sniffed the gloves. He placed gloves on his own hands. The rubber was flaccid where his short fingers ended. Using a scalpel, she cut into the bird at the nape of the neck, where the blood was. There was no time to have the boy apprentice. And anyway, he didn't ask to help. She peeled back the skin. Once the skin was separated from the body, she dipped it into a bowl of epoxy. *This is not long enough*, she thought. But she didn't care. She wanted to be done with this creepy four-foot-six killer. She gathered a mannequin made of wood and wool and wire. It had been intended for a finch, but she'd have to make it work. She stretched the skin over the faux body. Some of it sagged at the belly. The shape was off. The boy wouldn't notice. She reached into a box of clay eyes and purposely picked two mismatched ones. This boy didn't deserve her precision. She wrapped the bird's claws around a thick branch that looked like a magic wand. She shoved the bird on the branch and then onto the boy's chest.

"Here. Take it and go home." Nora transferred the bird to the boy.

The boy removed his gloves and left her studio without thanking her, heading back into the cold night.

Nora had second thoughts when she got back into bed. What if the boy got lost in the woods? What if he came across unsavory people on the road? But instead of going out to find him, she clenched her fleur-de-lis in her hands and counted backwards from one hundred until she fell asleep.

Outside, the boy was cold. He held on to his branch as he walked down the hill. He sniffed his left hand, searching for the latex smell. He lifted the bird. It didn't look right; its skin sagged further off the body with each step he took. His accuracy had surprised him when he used his slingshot to hurl the rock at the bird. He hadn't expected to hit it so hard. When he saw it was a blue jay, he was excited and then regretted that it wasn't something larger—a squirrel or an eagle.

The woman was no artist. What she'd handed him was more of a collage; a bird cobbled together in clunky pieces. He could probably have done it better himself. He imagined working on a swallow, then a turtle. He fantasized about making a fox of his own seem lifelike and then plunking marble eyes in a deer's eye sockets. The tools he had stolen—a scalpel, a bone cutter, and a knife—knocked against his body as he walked. He wondered how it might feel to peel back the skin of a one hundred and eighty-pound woman who was nothing but a stupid woodpusher.

# Bloodletting

———

## I.

The meteor crashed into a field five miles from the hospital where Shea was waking up from a double mastectomy.

Her brother, Clayton, breezed in carrying an array of colorful balloons.

"You going to a kid's birthday party?" asked Shea.

"These are for you."

Clayton tied the balloons to the guardrail of her hospital bed and sat on the vacant chair.

Shea yanked at a string until a violet balloon reached her face. She gently bit into the plastic and inhaled.

"Thank you," she said, her voice now an octave and a half higher.

"Inhaling helium isn't good for you," said Clayton.

"And cancer is?" challenged Shea, her voice still a bit higher than its original register.

Without Shea's prompting, Clayton turned on the TV. There was something about the sterility of a hospital room that invited everyone to take ownership of it.

A nurse bustled in to check Shea's stats.

Penny Peterson, blonde hair teased high, was reporting on the morning show. Young and fresh-faced, she looked like the poster girl for optimism. Shea hated her guts.

Clayton turned up the volume.

"Scientists say the asteroid was traveling at speeds of up to seventeen kilometers per second before making an impact near Cloudcroft, leaving a hole in the ground three storeys deep."

"Can you believe this?" The nurse, who had affixed various colorful cloth patches to her baggy pink scrubs, asked no one in particular. "Where'd it come down?"

"I don't know!" Clayton's eyes and mouth were opened wide like a hungry fish.

If Shea had had more strength and a fruit bowl in front of her, she would have tried to throw a grape into his mouth, a favorite fruit bowl pastime from their childhood.

Penny Peterson, as if on cue, answered the nurse's question.

"Baker's Field is known by many residents as 'The People's Field' and holds a weekly farmer's market."

"I've bought carrots there. For juicing. Overpriced." The nurse resumed her busy work.

"Turn it off," said Shea.

"But this is biggest thing to hit Cloudcroft!" Clayton stayed focused on the TV.

Shea knew Baker's Field. In high school, kids used to go there to make out and blast loud music through boom boxes. The meds confused her; she wasn't sure this was all really happening. She wasn't even sure she could feel her toes. Maybe they had accidentally removed more than they were supposed to. Hopeful Hearts was one of the best cancer-treatment centers in the nation, part of an effort to move recovery out of the hustle and bustle of big cities and into more aesthetically pleasing and slower-paced regions. But, maybe everyone was incompetent.

Penny explained that several cows were dead in the hole. Workers were awaiting a crane delivery from a neighboring town so they could haul them out, worried that dead cows would breed disease.

"What will become of this bovine bind? Stay tuned." Penny Peterson stared pensively into the camera, then the station cut to a commercial for bologna. Clayton turned off the TV as the surgical oncologist, Dr. Wheaton, came into the room.

"Is it supposed to hurt this much?" Shea asked as she tried to shift her position on the stiff hospital bed.

"Everything is fine." The doctor seemed confident.

"My breasts are gone."

Dr. Wheaton was here to discuss the psychological ramifications of mastectomies. Depression was common. She gave Shea a piece of paper with a number to call if things became too hard to handle. Shea imagined some big-bosomed woman answering the phone, spewing lines like, "I'm here for you." As soon as the doctor left the room, Shea would rip the piece of paper to shreds.

The balloons hovered above Shea's bed like birds floating on air currents. This time she chose a yellow one and reeled it in. She chomped into the latex and once again sucked in the helium.

"*Hirudo medicinalis. Hirudo medicinalis. Hirudo medicinalis,*" said Shea, like an incantation.

The doctor looked out of her element, as though "play" wasn't a common verb in her vocabulary.

Clayton laughed, "That's a good one! How in god's name did you remember that?"

"What does that mean?" asked Dr. Wheaton.

Shea was annoyed at the doctor's need to be involved.

"It's the Latin genus and species for leech," said Clayton.

"I should have recognized it was Latin," said the doctor.

"I'm in the leech industry," Clayton announced.

"You're making it sound like porn," said his sister. "Don't be modest. Clayton is a leech doctor."

"I've read about that," said Dr. Wheaton. "They suck the ailment out of you. Does it really work?"

"Does chemotherapy really work?" asked Clayton.

"Sometimes," said the doctor.

Was it the morphine haze or was her brother actually flirting with the doctor who removed her breasts? She hoped it was the drugs.

Shea pressed a button attached to a cord hanging beside her bed.

"What's that?" asked Clayton.

"For the pain. Ouch." She pressed the button again and smiled.

"But what is it?"

"Morphine. My very new best friend. Ouch," she pressed the button a third time, causing her brother to slide his palm over his face as though he were closing the eyes of a corpse. This had been a nervous habit of his since childhood. Her illness was out of his control and she knew this drove him nuts.

## II.

When Shea first returned to Cloudcroft, a month earlier, Clayton had seemed annoyed until she told him she had cancer. They sat in his leeching clinic, walls smelling of fresh paint as she explained to him that Dr. Wheaton wanted her to *act aggressively*. Chemotherapy. Radiation. The plan was to bombard her body and eradicate the cancer.

"But I thought I could begin with leeches," said Shea.

"Leeches aren't a miracle drug. They're just *Hirudo medicinalis*.

Shea was envious of the way the words slid off his tongue.

When he had finally relented, Shea began to hyperventilate.

"This is some homecoming." She'd watched, fascinated as her brother donned rubber gloves and pulled a liquid-filled jar from a shelf.

"Are those sterile?" she asked.

"Of course."

Shea grabbed an aquamarine glove from its cardboard box and blew into the opening at the bottom.

"How about now? Look! A turkey!" She squeezed the base of her turkey glove and trotted it around her face.

Clayton opened the screw top and poured the water into a sieve, catching the leeches. He lowered them so Shea could see them.

"Pretty little parasites," said Shea.

"Just a small prick. They actually anesthetize you before they start feeding."

"So *you* don't even have to do anything."

"If they could figure out how to run a business, they wouldn't even need me."

He placed a dark, slimy creature on her chest.

She felt the weight of it on her skin, but there was no penetration.

"I don't feel anything."

"Let me try another." He put the first leach back in the jar of water and grabbed a fresh one that was wriggling around the surface.

"Ouch!"

"It should hurt for only a second. Just a little sting and then the latch." Clayton continued to apply the leeches until Shea looked alien.

When he finished placing them on her body, Shea had tried to relax into the pulsating waves of the sucking. She imagined the leeches were little babies nursing at her teat. She pictured herself passing on her most valuable nourishment to them.

"Why couldn't it have been an original disease?" said Shea. "Everyone gets breast cancer," she said.

"They're getting bigger, see?"

Shea looked down; her leech babies had tripled in size.

"They still have a way to go," said Clayton.

She couldn't believe this was her brother's life—that this was a legitimate way to make money. She thought back to the two of them out in the yard, catching bugs in their mother's casserole dishes. He was supposed to have grown out of that phase.

After twenty minutes, Clayton began removing leeches with a pair of plastic tweezers.

"Okay, we're all done here."

"Do they go back in the water?" asked Shea.

"No, they go into alcohol."

"To get disinfected?"

"To die."

"That's cruel."

"Sharing leeches would be like sharing needles."

"But can't we save them and have them be my personal leeches? The only ones *I* use? Then it would be like me shooting up with my very own needle."

"It doesn't work that way," said Clayton.

Shea didn't care about leeching ethics. She just wanted results.

## III.

Shea picked at the grape leaves, part of the Greek takeout Clayton had brought home for dinner.

"Recovery is so boring." She ate a spoonful of hummus.

There was a loud crash from the hallway. Or was it outside?

"Another meteor?" Shea was shaken.

"Just the statue," her brother shouted from the hallway. "The left wing has been popping out."

Their parents had shipped home a kitschy replica of the Winged Victory statue after a trip to the Louvre. Over the years it had morphed into a coat rack.

In the kitchen, Clayton turned on the TV. Townies-turned-tourists jockeyed for position, aiming large lenses at the hole. Some clutched plastic binoculars. Helicopters hovered above. A mishmash of music blared through car speakers and people posed in front of "Danger" signs with thumbs up. Shea couldn't take anymore meteor talk. The scene behind the reporting newscaster was absurd. Carnivalesque. Vendors sold hot dogs and tacos. Homemade "Holy Pit!" t-shirts were on display. When Clayton went to rinse off his plate in the sink, Shea quickly pressed the button on the remote.

"Hey!! What are you doing? I was watching that."

"I'm sick of the pit. I'm sick of Penny Peterson," said Shea.

Clayton turned the TV back on. His house. His rules.

"Didn't you hear?" he asked. "One of the cows survived the impact. They've named her Isabelle. I've got to see this."

Of course. He was a man of science. He had to see empirical evidence in order to believe. Penny Peterson stood in front of the hole in the ground, her hair in a tight ponytail. She looked tired and a corner of her purple silk blouse had failed to stay fully tucked into her skirt. As she spoke, she tilted her head at various angles, pausing at adverbs before tilting her head in a new position.

"Isabelle the cow is being kept alive by a simple pulley and lever system. Food is carefully placed in this bucket and dropped down into the hole three times a day. Water is gently lowered six times a day. Isabelle's owner is eager to have her out and back to pasture. After suffering the loss of several of his cows, he appreciates the show of support from around the world. Officials say they are working on a way to lift Isabelle back up to safety, and caring communities as far away as India are holding prayer vigils for the cow that survived catastrophe. What will become of this cow conundrum? Stay tuned."

The news just reported disaster, but did nothing to intervene.

Little dramas were occurring all around Shea. Just this morning she had watched from the kitchen window as a jay struggled to catch a large moth on the other side of the fence. Each time the jay seemed to have his meal secured in his mouth, the moth would escape. It was hard for her not to root for the underdog and when the bird finally captured its catch, she couldn't help but feel a deep sadness.

Shea and Clayton ate their lamb kabobs in silence.

After a series of commercials showcasing an all-in-one titanium home gym, an anti-snoring mouth guard, and reduced airfare on flights to Cloudcroft, Penny Peterson's face again loomed on the television. Stray hairs escaped her tight ponytail. Her mascara ran down her face in the rain. But she continued to report, hands slightly shaking as she spoke: "We've just received breaking news: a possible radiation leak has been detected at the meteor crash sight. It has long been believed that meteors have the capacity to emit low doses of radiation, but this hypothesis has been refuted in the past. Experts from the Institute of Foreign Objects have concluded that there is indeed a danger of radiation poisoning and have closed the site to the public until further notice. What will become of this radioactive riddle?"

## IV.

It wasn't the circus atmosphere that drew Shea to the pit. Not the little girl who spilled her tub of kettle corn when her mother jerked her away. Nor was it the uniformed guards aggressively escorting people away from the area surrounding the pit. And not even the man who fought to retrieve his camera from a government worker.

It was the close-up at the end of Penny's news segment. Isabelle the cow was lying down, mooing desperately. Her eyes looked as if they were going to pop out of their sockets. Her tongue lolled, like a chameleon who had fallen asleep while trying to catch a bug.

*This is what survival looks like,* Shea had thought.

Reports of a massive radiation leak didn't scare her away. She had been through radiation. She hadn't melted. And she didn't have to worry about her reproductive organs being zapped; they were already ruined. The surgery hadn't worked. She was slated for chemo anyway. Why not get a jump-start, au natural?

At the crash site she ignored the "Keep Out" and "Danger" signs and crossed the caution tape without hesitation. The site was abandoned. A desolate fairground littered with flyers, popcorn, and soda cups. Disaster was a cheap and fleeting form of entertainment.

There, in the crater below her, was Isabelle, the forlorn cow who spent her day ambling around the hole with her four stomachs growling from hunger pangs.

*So much for heroes,* thought Shea. Officials who had just a few days earlier stated they would do *whatever* they could to help Isabelle out of the hole had left town with their families, fearing emission damage.

She recalled how the newspaper had explained that the meteor might have actually jolted the earth off its axis. She now stood on ground that was at a slightly different angle than before. This was the kind of incident that could alter everything.

Rocks, the color of rawhide, surrounded the field, fragments of the landed meteor.

Shea walked slowly. Her body still felt foreign to her post-surgery—as though she were inhabiting new skin—a hermit crab that had left its shell but hadn't yet found a new one.

Shea approached the hole and pulled out a pair of binoculars she had brought from home. She focused her eyes on the mound of weakening flesh in the northern-most part of the hole. Isabelle's tail was swishing at a legato pace.

She ducked under the rope and approached the edge of the hole, lowering herself to keep her balance, not wanting her life to end with a stupid, careless slip. She concentrated on keeping her feet firmly on the ground as she leaned as far over the hole as she could, then fell to her hands and knees, then down to her stomach. Her chest felt raw as it scraped across the uneven earth. Her tissues still working hard to regenerate.

"Hey, I have something for you. It's not much, just some grass from our lawn. Actually, it's from the neighbor's lawn, the grass on our side doesn't grow because my brother is incapable of tending to it." Shea also brought painkillers for herself, but decided to share. She wrapped three pills in the clump of grass before throwing it down into the hole.

The cow began to moo, the sound echoing up the earthy walls. She stirred and ambled toward the meager offering.

A mild breeze blew and Shea thought about the invisible waves purportedly passing through the air. She tried to see them. Radiation, surfing on wind currents.

Lactation. This cow's raison d'être as far as the farmers were concerned. And something Shea would now never experience. She knew she couldn't save the cow, not without superpowers. But she didn't want it to suffer alone either. They could comfort each other.

"I'll be back, cow." Shea said as she heaved herself up from the warm dirt. She wasn't sure if she meant at the pit or in some sort of afterlife where they were both headed.

As Shea returned to her car, from out of the dust appeared Penny Patterson, hair down, blowing wildly, like Medusa's snakes, microphone in hand, followed by a cameraman in a protective orange bodysuit.

Penny ran up to Shea and clutched her arm tightly.

"May I interview you?"

Shea nodded.

"Why are you here?"

"I had to see her."

"Honey, I'm leaving," the impatient cameraman said to Penny, whose face had broken out with small patches of stress-induced psoriasis or perhaps radiation acne.

"You can't just leave me alone out here!" Penny's voice quivered.

Shea had her own question, "Why are you still here?"

Penny, unlike the cow, wasn't stuck in a hole.

"It's in my contract." A lone tear rolled down Penny's cheek.

## V.

"We need to make a plan to leave," Clayton announced two days after the radiation proclamation.

"But I just got settled," said Shea.

"You have to be willing to change."

After dinner, Shea and Clayton gathered all the necessary materials in the bathroom to remove the bandages around Shea's chest.

"I can handle this on my own, you know." Shea took off her shirt and looked at herself in the mirror.

"But I'm here. I want to help," said Clayton.

Too tired to fight, she let her brother locate the end of the cloth, tucked in and attached with a metal grip. He undid it and began to unravel the beige material from around her torso, as she stood poised in first position. An ancient rite of de-mummification. He unwound the bandage around and around her body.

"Let me try turning," Shea ordered and she began to spin ever so slowly, like a spool of thread unraveling. "I'm like a pig on a spit!" Shea laughed.

She knew Clayton thought she laughed a little too much. He probably wanted her to take all this more seriously—the cancer, the recovery, the radiation spilling over the town.

Shea was still rotating.

"Aren't you getting dizzy?" asked Clayton.

She stopped turning as the last of the bandage unpeeled itself from her skin, revealing soiled gauze.

"This is disgusting," said Shea.

"This is how science works," Clayton said, but before he could extract the sterilized medical tongs from their packaging, she stripped the gauze off with her fingers. She squinted at her reflection in the mirror.

"I look like a boy."

"No you don't."

He was supposed to say that.

She pulled away. "I don't think it's a bad thing. Boys have it easier. Don't you think?"

Clayton stayed silent. She thought he was worried about getting into a conversation about gender equality, worried his sister couldn't handle it in her "fragile" state. Shea thought this was ironic, since she felt stronger now than she ever had in her entire life.

Her brother soaked cotton balls with alcohol, which Shea ran along the lines of the stitching. "Make sure you get it everywhere," he instructed.

It looked dramatic, her chest, red lines raised, black stitching thread exposed.

"What do you think they did with my breasts?"

"I don't know. Put them in the hazardous waste container, I guess."

"I hope so. Those were some hazardous breasts."

Clayton wiped his hands over his face.

"Do you have a problem talking about my breasts?"

"Your doctor called to check in on you. She asked what our evacuation plan was. She asked me out for a drink," said Clayton.

Nothing could be just hers. Not her doctor. Not her body. Just the cancer—no one wanted to claim that.

The next day, after a labored afternoon walk around the deserted neighborhood, Shea came home to a message scrawled on a paper grocery bag left hanging on the Winged Victory statue.

*We have to leave. It's not safe here. Went to office to feed leeches. Then home. Told Dr. Wheaton we could give her a lift. Be ready and packed when I get home.*

*—C*

Let her doctor take her seat in the car next to her brother, she didn't care. She had to get back to the cow.

Shea looked up at the Winged Victory statue, its stub of left shoulder angled a bit out of place.

"Stupid amputee," she mumbled and picked up her car keys.

Clayton's office building was empty and there was an eerie silence while she went into the elevator and up to the sixth floor. His office was empty. Shea looked up at the large poster of a magnified leech on the wall of the waiting room. She was relieved that leeches were small creatures.

She opened the door of the examination room and to her surprise, she found her brother, naked on the table, covered in leeches, looking like someone had glued large black jellybeans all over his chest. His eyes were closed, in a state of such ecstasy that even in her shock, she didn't want to interrupt him. *Intimacy like this shouldn't be disturbed.*

Shea tried to picture what he must be feeling—imagined the blood leaving his body and filling up the leeches like air in a balloon—imagined them floating up, bellies full of his helium-blood until they floated away, into a tree. The sky. Another planet.

Clayton opened his eyes and met Shea's.

"What are you doing here?"

"I came to tell you that I'm not coming with you."

"What are you doing here!" he repeated frantically.

"We all have something to hide. Don't be embarrassed," she said consolingly.

"Get out of here!!"

"I love you, Clayton. Thank you for everything."

"Just leave!"

A large jar of leeches sat on the table. "May I take these?" Shea asked.

Clayton anxiously picked the animals off his skin. She could tell it hurt.

Shea took the jar and left as her brother muttered, "Stupid suckers."

## VI.

Even though there were no other cars on the road, Shea obeyed the traffic lights as she drove through the barren streets back to the pit. The jar of leeches sat in the seat next to her. Like sailors on rough seas, the leeches swayed back and forth with the movement of the car. The scene at the pit now seemed more desperate than when she had left it. It was completely deserted. The rope that had surrounded the massive hole had been removed, perhaps to be used as a noose by a religious fanatic who believed that the meteor landing and then leaking radiation signaled the beginning of Armageddon.

Penny Patterson lay on the ground next to a "Caution" sign a few feet from the hole. Her cracked blue lips slightly parted as though she had been interrupted, uttering something important. Microphone wire snaked out to nowhere. Shea knelt down and put her palm in front of Penny's mouth to feel for her breath. She was dead.

Shea scratched her arm, which had been itching for days. Both arms were red, dry, and swollen. She wondered if the surgeon should have cut them off as well.

Isabelle's food supply had dwindled to a clump of loose weeds. Through her binoculars, Shea could see the animal's bones protruding from her haunches. Shea wished she had the strength to heave her out of there—superhero strength to swoop and clutch the cow in gigantic talons and carry her to safety.

Shea pushed the heavy glass jar up to the edge of the pit, positioning herself so that she was over Isabelle, who leaned against the side of the hole. She unscrewed the metal lid, then tipped the jar and watched as first water, then a cascade of leeches spilled over the edge, freefalling.

Thirty feet below, the cow shifted, surprised by the cold water, and she turned her weary head behind her and saw the assemblage of leeches dragging themselves over her sagging skin. At first she thought her own spots were moving, changing forms, but when she succumbed to the intense piercing all over her body, she exhaled and allowed herself to feel comfort at the touch of other living beings.

# Plush

————

It's all about the costume.

I wrap my fuzzy arms around the stranger and hold on tight. Have to put a cap on the time I'm allotting for each hug because tonight, there's a long line. Not surprising since I am the top Cuddler at the CLUB. Ranked number one for four months straight.

They don't know what I look like underneath the yards of sewn fleece and shaggy mane; my wiry frame, oily hair, and adolescent complexion are safe.

Here, I am not Tristan.

Here, I am Lion.

It doesn't get better than this.

I blame the Salvation Army, but I guess it's really Mom's fault. She's the one who donated my costume to them in the first place. She must have thought it was from some Halloween back when we were kids. I had been hiding it in a box in the garage to keep the whole thing under wraps, but Mom threw it in the garbage bag with the rest of the donations: scratched Teflon pans, an old domino set, my sister's miniature glass pony collection, a pair of Winchester roller skates, a bunch of musty books, and clothing. Lots of clothing, including my work uniform.

It *was* all about the costume, which is now probably at some sorting facility somewhere, being evaluated and distributed to a store where it will be bought for $4.99 by some fool who smells like alcohol.

Just my luck.

"I feel so good about myself today," Mom says, fox stole around her thick, dewlapped neck. The thing looks like it was roadkill. She should have donated it with the rest of her shit.

I give her a fake smile. Two more months in this dump and then I'm out of here. I'll be a high-school graduate with the beginnings of a savings account, ready to face the world. If it were up to Mom, she'd have me live in this house forever. Dad has big plans for me to join the army. Not wanting me to get a job is their way of controlling my future.

My sister Mavis sits at the table trying to balance a spoon on the edge of her nose. Earlier this morning, before I'd realized that Mom had donated my lion suit, I tore Mavis's room apart—she's my twin.

"Such a coincidence that we had twins because their grandma was a twin," Mom always tells people.

"That's not a coincidence, that's genetics," I used to say, but I just gave up.

Instead of finding my costume in Mavis's room, there was something else hidden under her bed. Paperwork. For a volunteer position in Ghana. To be an art teacher at a school for girls. She'd already filled out the application. I won't rat her out. I want to be there when she tells our folks she's leaving and the shit hits the fan.

Mavis pours herself a bowl of Frosty-Os. I tell her all the sugar is bad for her acne, but she doesn't listen. She never eats what the rest of us are having—boiled turkey omelets this morning. Dad peels the skin away from the flesh with his fork and it comes off in one piece. The limp flap looks like it could be a cape for an action figure. Super Turkey Skin: inflates his wattle to epic proportions before clawing evildoers in a single bound! Dad passes the skin to Mom who, making her way toward the kitchen, pretends first to offer it to the fox around her neck before putting it in her own mouth. Mavis takes sugar from the pink-and-white box in front of her and sprinkles it on top of the contents of her bowl, like it's snowing.

"My drawing is one of the finalists for the school t-shirt." Mavis spoons the O's one at a time—her mild case of OCD on display.

"Math quiz today. Gonna ace it," I say.

Dad merely nods at our offerings and stuffs his eggs in his mouth.

"Say something, my dears?" Mom asks, joining us at the table.

Mavis and I look at one another. I shake my head and she murmurs, "Never mind." Dad was never really one to offer praise. I'd tell him I raised the most money in my class for our adopt-a-family and he would say the school should be paying me for all my hard work.

"So what are you two doing after school?" It's Friday, which means we don't have to rush straight home. Dad doesn't like us going out. It's not like he wants us to stay home and have game night or anything like that. He lets me out if I'm doing something "respectable" like going to the library, and he allows Mavis to go to the mall with the girls once in a while. We get around his rules by combining our only two options: lying and sneaking out.

"I don't know. Maybe mall time." Mavis slurps her milk, which makes Mom twitch.

"That's nice," Dad adds. "You and the girls. How's Lonnie doing? Her father used to work at that bank that went belly up, poor guy."

Dad's been a refrigerator repairman his whole life. It's what his dad did. Before that, his grandfather was in the icebox business and his great-grandfather worked with dehydrators and crocks. Dad likes to lecture us about "work ethic." Mom comes from old money that no longer exists. She was raised in some mansion with wait service. She likes to tell Dad how they had three refrigerators, one downstairs, and one upstairs, and one by the pool. But Grandfather was apparently involved in some "shady business" and lost it all in "one fell swoop," forcing the family to pack up whatever they could carry in one leather suitcase in the middle of the night and vacate the premises, the town, the entire east coast. Mom was wearing the fox the night they left.

She brings in a pile of zucchini pancakes stacked ten high. I growl at her fox stole as she puts the plate on the table. The fox's face flops uncomfortably close to mine. She doesn't like to take that thing off. She claims it's because she has poor circulation, and don't even try to sell her on scarves. She says they're porous. Mom leans down and places one finger on my sister's shoulder and closes her eyes as she speaks.

"My little girl. All grown up. You can vote. Be your own person."

"Let's not rush into things," says Dad.

"You can make a porno," I say, encouragingly.

"Oh, Tristan. Do you have to be so vulgar all the time?"

Apparently, it's not vulgar when Dad tells me I should be a soldier. Apparently, it's the only decent job prospect I have. His fridge business has been dwindling. He says the only way I can afford to go to college is if I join the army. Fighting isn't my thing. I don't feel an obligation to defend my country. I can't walk down the school halls without getting the middle finger from someone. That's what I'm supposed to fight for?

Dad explores his gums with an orange toothpick. When he finds something stuck, he makes this grotesque sucking noise and then swallows.

We reach for the syrup at the same time. I inadvertently grasp his hand, which is wrapped around the neck of the plastic bottle. His skin is cold: what you'd expect from a man who spends all day placing them in sub-zero temperatures. It's the first body contact we've had since I can remember. I quickly let go. He was there first.

After school, when I tell Captain Kevin my costume is no longer, he hangs his head and sighs. He puts his hand on my shoulder.

"You had a good run, Cuddler 82. I didn't want to see you go out like this."

It's true. The proof is on the leader board at company headquarters, a large basement warehouse under our town's mall. There's no sign anywhere advertising what we do, but every so often a wayward consumer will wander down the elevator, hopped up on a rush of shopping adrenalin, and ask what we sell. They're usually sent back to Kevin. He checks them out and decides if they seem like the type who would want to join. He looks for longing in their eyes. Otherwise he lies and says the basement floor is the maintenance team.

"But don't you think it's not only about the costume?" I say. I mean, I work hard to engage the people. It's all about having an affable attitude. About being open. It has to go beyond the plush.

Kevin puts his finger up and disappears into a back closet marked "Captains Only." He returns with a turkey suit on a hanger.

"It's all about the costume." Kevin pushes the suit toward me.

"Don't you have anything a little more, you know . . . lovable?"

He raises his eyebrows.

I take the suit.

So this is how it works. Kevin sends out an e-mail to all those on the list of patrons interested in coming to a Cuddle Party. The list has been compiled from people who have attended before, or else friends of friends e-mail Kevin. Sometimes, he'll send scouts out into the mall to discreetly recruit customers.

A couple of days after the e-mail goes out, Kevin puts together a list of the RSVPs. The day before the Cuddle Party, he sends another e-mail with directions to the secret location. There have been Cuddle Crashers before, so it's important he doesn't reveal the party's location until the last minute. Of course, Cuddlers find out a week ahead of time. Some participants make certain requests for which Cuddlers they want at the party. Just for the record, I was always requested. We'll see how much they like hugging a fucking turkey. "Come nuzzle in close with this North American patriotic bird that tastes good between two slices of bread and slathered in gravy. Oh and it can't even pull it together enough to fly!"

Dinner is a mealy pot of corn beef hash with fried eggs on top that look like eyes. Mavis noshes on Choco-Puffs. Mom offers Mavis's uneaten portion to the fox stole, nestled as usual between her hair and neck. A ten-year-old gag.

"I'll just leave it on the table if you change your mind."

Guess the fox isn't hungry tonight.

It's Mavis's turn to be on duty. She'll stay home and be on call to make an excuse for me in case our parents come looking while I sneak out. I'll take tomorrow. Thank God these parties are at night or I'd never get past my folks. Outside the window of our Jack-and-Jill bathroom is a large ash tree, perfect for getting us safely down to the street. It's a system that's worked great over the last year, minus that one time I accidentally locked her out during a snowstorm. Part of the reason it works so well is that I don't always hold up my end of the bargain. If I know there's a Cuddle Party happening, I make it my business to be there. Every penny counts. I just have to be sure and get home before she does.

Mavis spent the afternoon with friends from school finishing up a knitting project that Mom got her started on weeks ago: soda cozies. Mom thinks it's going to be a cash cow. I don't bother to ask her why anyone would want something that actually makes soda warmer.

I've been doing laundry and resting up for my big coming out as a turkey at the Cuddle Party tonight. I finally get around to greasing the track on the window, too. It's been making this awful squeaking sound when either of us slides it open. Mavis hasn't said anything, but I'm pretty sure she has a boyfriend. She's been asking me to cover for her a lot more than usual lately, and at school, I sometimes see her eating with this Conor kid from her math class. Dad would hate him—always chewing gum and brandishing hair long enough to tuck behind his ears.

Dad sits at the table reading the paper.

"Anything interesting, dear?" asks Mom.

"War moved," he grumbles. He's been obsessed with war news ever since this whole thing broke out years ago. Part of the reason he wants me to join the army, I'm sure. He'd join himself if he weren't so old, so instead, he's willing to sacrifice me.

"Where did it go?" Mom rearranges the dying white peonies in a vase on the table. They're starting to give off that sweet stench that makes everything taste like rotten flowers.

"North by northeast. Into jungle territory. It's a whole new game now. Says here the highlights will be on channel four tonight. Nine o'clock. Remind me."

After dinner, we help Mom clear the table. Dad is already planted on his rocker, waiting for nine o'clock to roll around. I think we both feel kind of guilty having to lie to Mom when we go out, so we try hard to help her out after meals. We form an assembly line. After the table is cleared, Mavis washes the dishes, I dry them, and Mom oversees the process, wicking away any overlooked droplets with the fox's tail.

Tonight, the Cuddle Party is at ten o'clock, at Gia Smith's house on Pine and 24th. I slide my crumpled bill in the slot and grab my change. It's my job to arrive there in uniform. But I don't like taking buses in full regalia. Taxis are hit and miss. One cabbie begged me to come to his daughter's third birthday party the next day. He said he'd let me have a beer and take a swing at the piñata. Most cabs drive right by. I've changed in public-park bathrooms, department-store dressing rooms, and once behind an installation at the Modern Museum of Art entitled, "Disney on Crack." The docents thought I was part of the exhibit.

I couldn't stomach Mom's hash, so before changing I grab a bite to eat at Stellar Burger. The suit is heavy, stuffed inside one of Mom's donation garbage bags.

"I'll have one Busy Bee meal, please." (Four buns alternating with three patties and lots of mustard.)

"Side of regular fries or garlic?"

"Garlic."

A kid with the beginnings of a moustache punches in my order.

"Actually, plain fries."

"Have a date?" he asks.

"Oh, yeah."

He lifts his hands and gives me two thumbs up with a side of crooked smile.

"Avoid halitosis," is Rule No. 5 in the Cuddle Manual, a hand-stamped packet covered in a red fuzzy binding.

After sliding the remains on my purple tray in the trash, I go to the restroom, dragging my bag behind me. I feel like Santa Claus. An old guy using the urinal looks at me when I enter the bathroom. His urine comes out in spurts, like he has something to hide. I change in the handicapped stall; it's the only one that will accommodate my big bag. The sporadic dribbles from the old man come to a halt as I take off my clothes and open the bag. It looks like the remnants of a turkey that shed its skin and waddled toward the nearest coop. I pick up the deflated animal and inspect it.

Shit.

The zipper is in the back. Major design flaw and something all Cuddlers complain about.

I leave my socks on. You never know what the A/C is going to be like at the places we go to. And it's not like you can ask them to change it. That's Rule No. 2 in the Cuddle Manual: "The only thing Cuddlers can say at a Cuddle Party is 'yes' in response to a client's cuddle request. Please be sure and learn the sign for 'I have to go to the bathroom.'" I've never been docked points for talking, but others have. And docked points equals docked pay. We work on commission. Cindee Carter was suspended for a week for asking a client where she got her shoes.

This turkey cloth is itchier than my last costume. Cheap material. I'll have to buy a spandex suit to wear underneath. Stepping into the red tights, I slide the coarse fabric over my body. My arms enter the wings, which are missing a noticeable amount of feathers. I put the turkey head on and exit the bathroom stall to take a look at my new persona.

Old guy is washing his hands. Just the tips of his fingers, really. He stops what he's doing and looks at me. I hope he isn't going to have a heart attack.

"Zip me up?" I turn so my back is facing him. After drying his fingers on his pants he walks over, fiddles with the zipper until it catches, then moves it up my back to the base of my neck.

"Want me to do the eye hook as well?"

I practice nodding like a turkey would nod. Small but deliberate movements. He fastens the hook and then gives me a gentle pat on the back as though to say, "All done."

I thank him and wave good-bye, though my worn appendage won't rise as high as I'd like.

I look at myself in the mirror, head on, then profile. My beak isn't even made out of shiny plastic. It's felt. And it droops, like an elephant's trunk. Or a compass, pointing south.

Gia Smith's home is only a few blocks away from the burger joint. I've strategically planned this. People stare at me on the street. I bet they assume I started the day with a stack full of colorful flyers in my hand for the latest sandwich-shop special or some Save the Environment campaign. When I was a lion, people on the street would slap me five. They'd want to pose with me and take my picture. They'd try to usher me into the bar to buy me a beer. "Please arrive at all Cuddle Parties in costume, ready to begin work," and "Your real identity is to remain a secret at all times," are rules No. 3 and 4. They want this to be an authentic experience for participants.

I was one of those wayward kids who wandered into the offices in the basement of the mall over a year ago. Maybe it was my habit of standing really close to the person I'm talking to that clued Captain Kevin in to the fact that I'd make an ideal Cuddler.

"You want a great way to make some extra cash?"

I nodded. Who wouldn't?

He invited me to spend that night at a Cuddle Party, not as an employee, but as a participant. At first I was self-conscious when I entered the host's apartment, but everyone was so kind. Monkey was there (who knew I'd be working with him a year later?) and gave me my first hug. I could have stayed there all night. Mikey, tonight's supervisor, later explained the biological reaction people have to hugging, the intense release of endorphins.

"It's better than any drug," he said.

I was hooked.

A husky bouncer at the new locale looks me up and down. He's there to deal with guests who drink too much. I tell the doorman tonight's passwords, "phantom limb." He waves me in.

Inside I see Bunny, Monkey, and Chick standing around talking. Most Cuddlers use their real voice when in costume, but Chick masks hers with this high-pitched, fake baby voice. It's kinda cute. I don't know any of their real names or what they actually look like, as we all strictly adhere to Rule No. 4 and even show up at staff meetings in costume.

"You new?" asks Bunny.

I go to put both arms on my hips, but my wings won't budge. "Are you kidding? It's me!"

Monkey tries to peer through the mesh area hiding my face.

"Lion?" Monkey asks. "What happened to you?"

"Costume's disappeared."

"How the mighty have fallen," says Bunny. "Looks like I have a good chance of sweeping the leader board tonight!" He high-fives Monkey.

Chick puts her wing on my shoulder. "Sorry."

She's always been nice to me.

"I hear we're going have a full turnout tonight." Chick brushes her yellow leggings with her wings. She's one of the few who has any actual body shape exposed, although now I've joined her with my turkey legs. The rest of the Cuddlers are all hidden in their oversized costumes. Her costume is made out of real feathers, unlike mine. The friction from all that hugging means she loses a lot of yellow feathers each night and she says she has to buy bags of new ones and glue them on after almost every party.

Mikey bounces into the room.

"Who do we have here? New Cuddler?" he asks me and comes over to shake my wing.

"It's Lion! Can you believe this shit?" Monkey says.

"Wow!" Mikey looks stunned. "I don't know what to say. Okay,

Cuddlers, I want you all to gather in a circle. Our clients will start coming in a few minutes, and I want to debrief you on the situation."

A puppy and kangaroo I don't know join the circle.

"So, tonight we have mostly return clients, but we do have two new ones, so we're gonna have to go ahead with the Rules Circle."

In middle school I was in a play once. I had what you'd call a supporting role, playing an organ grinder, but before each show, we'd get in a circle and our drama teacher, Mrs. Passomanik, would talk about what a great performance this was going to be and how much she appreciated us. Dad made me quit drama after that one show. He said the army wasn't looking to recruit thespians.

The Circle before Cuddle Parties is similar to Mrs. Passomanik's. Mikey lets us know if we have any returning clientele, and if they've made any special requests for specific Cuddlers. The energy in the room is electric. We are ready to begin our work.

Cuddlers begin the evening on the periphery waiting to be approached by someone looking for a hug. Once we've doled out our first hug, we can circulate. I lean against the wall and wait and watch.

My first night as a turkey was mediocre. It was at least forty-five minutes before anyone asked for a hug. As Lion, I was heavily pursued. When lines would form, my fans would head to the back of the line for seconds. Tonight, I wanted to pound my chest and shout out, "I'm really Lion! It's me!" Chick seems to have taken the lead. Probably because Easter is just around the corner.

The adrenalin has worn off considerably by the time my bus pulls to a stop. With my costume double-bagged and stuffed in my backpack, I get off the bus and walk the two blocks to my house. The rain has stopped, which means I'll need to be extra quiet sneaking back into my room.

I hoist myself up to the window and try to slide the cold glass up. It's locked. I'm going to kill my sister. I'm exhausted. All I want to do is find a good hiding place for my costume and crawl into bed.

I knock lightly on the window.

Nothing.

I tap a little louder, using my fingernails to drum the William Tell Overture on the glass. My sister responds to rhythm. She opens the window.

"What the fuck?"

"Sorry, I fell asleep."

She takes my bag as I climb through the window, the TV still broadcasting the war downstairs where Dad has, no doubt, fallen asleep.

In the morning, when Mom leans down to pour orange juice into my empty mug, the fox's nose touches the inside of my ear.

"They lost a nuke." Dad startles me, rattling his paper with fervor.

"Who did?" Mom brings in the boiled eggs as Mavis has a seat with a box of Choco-Puffs and gives me the middle finger while no one is looking.

"We did. In the jungle. They have trained monkeys over there. It's the new biological warfare."

"The monkeys stole the bomb?" Mavis adds a handful of marshmallows to her cereal.

"Monkeys are smart," I say, trying to get in on the conversation.

"Yeah, smarter than you," adds Mavis.

"Hey, I did so well I threw the entire curve off for the math test yesterday." I look at my dad.

"Damn monkeys," he says, his blue-and-white striped union suit unbuttoned at the top so that his scraggly, gray chest hair sits like an unmowed patch of grass.

"What are you two going to do today?" asks Mom.

"Mall."

"Homework at the library."

"That's nice."

The next week, we're at a posh brownstone on Circle Road. It's a nice neighborhood—a whole lot nicer than the one I live in. The owners, Frank and Gretchen, have hosted before. They make it a point to serve their own appetizers—things like fried calamari and chicken satay with peanut dipping sauce in addition to the usual veggies and dip and waffled potato chips. Even though the last time wasn't a shining moment in my cuddling career, I'm optimistic that I can transform my new status as a turkey into something desirable—after all, beneath all the fake feathers and polyester, it's still just me.

It was my turn to stay at home tonight so that Mavis could go out, probably with that Conor joker. I let her have a ten-minute lead, just in case she forgot something and had to come home, before checking that Mom was asleep and Dad was flaked out in front of the TV. Then I made my escape out the window and down the tree.

Mikey pulls me aside and says I have to do something with my limp beak before people show up. I ask him what I'm supposed to do, but he shrugs and says, "Get creative." Doesn't he know that turkeys aren't right-brain kind of creatures?

"I'll be back," I tell Chick and the gang. Chick shakes her hips back and forth. She gets all amped up before a party.

Outside, the cold seeps through the mesh fabric in front of my mouth. I inhale deeply and see my breath rise. Why couldn't I have been a peacock or a penguin? How to fix my beak?

Two blocks from the house there's a laundromat and a deli and, across the street, a liquor store. The rest of the businesses look closed. Evening commuters honk at me as I jaywalk toward the liquor store. I give them the middle finger under my wing.

It dawns on me that in this roomier disguise I might be able to get away with breaking Rule No. 7: "No alcohol is to be consumed by employees while attending a Cuddle Party." Maybe a few sips would take the edge off and help me get my groove back.

I don't know what I'm looking for to help fix my beak, but I'll know it when I see it. What would Mavis do in this situation? She's the artist in the family, after all. I picture her in Ghana with a bunch of kids sitting around and making batik t-shirts. She'd find a way to make this beak look good stuffed with grass or cotton balls.

In the liquor store, a guy next to me holds out two bottles. "Which do you think? Cabernet or Chardonnay?"

"What are you having for dinner?" I ask. He looks surprised, like he thought I wouldn't talk.

"Chicken. Hope that doesn't offend you." He laughs and looks at his girlfriend.

"Cabernet," I say. That bottle looks more interesting, abstract statuesque bodies interwoven like they're participating in a Greek orgy.

The checker hears our conversation and decides to butt in.

"You're supposed to have white wine with bird," says the checker.

The guy holding the bottle shrugs. "I'm going with the turkey on this one."

Toward the front of the store is an assortment of mini liquor bottles. I pick out three: tequila, gin, and vodka and set them on the counter.

"Is that packaging?" I point to the pile of shredded paper behind the counter, hoping to distract the checker from remembering to check my ID.

"Sure is."

"Mind if I take some? For my beak?" I shake my head to emphasize my dilemma. My limp beak jiggles back and forth. "Oh, and I'll take these three bottles as well."

The checker rings me up and passes me a handful of shredded paper.

If I don't get back for the ringing of the opening triangle, I'm out for the evening. It's in our contract.

Outside I take my head off and place two of the bottles down my left wing. I swig the tequila and then tightly stuff the paper into my beak. Voilà.

Back inside Mikey is orienting first-timers to the routine while a few guests stand around the food table, sipping wine and chewing on vegetable sticks. He's good at gathering people in circles and making them follow directions. He used to be a preschool teacher.

"Looking better, Turkey." Mikey puts his hand on my shoulder and

squeezes. He unwraps a triangle from a cloth bandana and strikes it with
the metal rod three times. Tonight I'm brimming with optimism and
tequila. I will play the part of a confident, flightless bird. I will be desired.

Chick is approached quickly by a guy, probably in his mid-forties,
wearing a polo shirt. He leans in for a hug and Chick embraces him. I can
see she waits for him to release before she removes her wings from him.
Soon, most Cuddlers are hard at work. In fact, everyone is, except for
me.

Swaying back and forth, shifting my weight from one turkey foot to
the next, I anxiously wait.

Mikey has his lifeguard whistle around his neck. He's never had to
use that thing, but it's always there.

I feel invisible.

Heading toward the bathroom, I open the vodka, drink it, and return
to my post.

A woman walks my way, looking as though she might approach me.
I raise a wing to entice her, but she turns away at the last minute and
grabs a piece of jicama off the table. I've had it. I don't even bother to
excuse myself as I remove and then unscrew the cap off the third bottle.
No one can see what I'm doing under my costume. I'm hoping I look like
I'm just scratching an itch.

Chick is facing me from across the room. Maybe she's looking at me,
but it's hard to say because I can't see her eyes. I wave. She waves back,
but we get interrupted by a large woman who asks her for a cuddle. The
woman's shoulders are bobbing up and down. She's crying. She must
have had some sort of release. It's not uncommon at these parties. The
contact can be so "emotionally awakening," as Mikey says. It's the same
reason people get dogs—to have someone to snuggle with. We never
had any pets growing up. Dad said they demand too much affection.

Mavis swears that we used to have a pet fox that looked exactly like
the one wrapped around my mother's neck, but I have no memory of
this. Mavis says there used to be pictures in the photo album of us all
around the Christmas tree, Dad drinking a Bloody Mary out of a coffee
mug (Mavis assumed this because of the celery sticking out of it) and

the fox, curled up in an empty present box, but when she went to show me the evidence, the photo was gone.

As Chick wraps her wings around the woman, I watch her body swaying from side to side. Chick can be so maternal.

People have loosened up and are now moving away from us Cuddlers toward each other. It's the ultimate goal—transferring the safety and trust of a plushie to regular people, so that casual smiles and hellos on the street to strangers can be replaced by much-needed embraces. We've been at war for as long as I can remember; apparently monkeys are losing deadly weapons of mass destruction. I mean, who doesn't need a hug?

Chick makes her way past a line of guests and ends up next to me. The feathers on her upper right shoulder look ruffled from the onslaught of that large woman's tears.

Maybe it's the alcohol warming me up from the inside, but I am hyper-aware of Chick standing within close proximity. I want her closer.

"You smell nice," I whisper.

"Rule No. 2," she says back. She takes her job seriously. Another thing I like about her.

The drink goes to my head.

I look down at Chick's round calves. "You also have nice legs."

"Ew," Chick says.

Have I disgusted her so much that she's willing to break the rules?

She leans in and sniffs me, and then crosses one wing on top of the other, scolding me. I try to put my wing up to my beak, asking for her silence, but it doesn't reach. I'm too late and she walks away.

I stare at the grain in the hardwood floor and then contemplate my turkey feet.

"Cuddle me?"

Finally, the words I've been waiting to hear all night. I look up to survey the turkey-loving Cuddler. It's my father. Still dressed in his refrigerator-repairman suit, a newspaper wedged under his arm.

My body freezes as he comes in for a hug. The paper falls to the floor. His arms wrap around my shoulders and meet at the small of my back.

He rests his head on my wattle and squeezes, mildly at first, and then he tightens his grip. I can hear a faint cooing sound coming out of his mouth, like a happy baby.

It's the first hug he's given me in years.

I squeeze back, eager to make a connection. I want to shout, "Dad, it's me!" and make a big reveal. But then I grow resentful. He doesn't know who he is hugging. He'd rather embrace a stranger than his own son. In fact, he's willing to pay for it.

My grip tightens as he moves to let go. I am owed much more than this—much more. He is not getting off so easily. I feel his back pulling against my arms.

The smell of coolant reaches my nose.

"Hey," he says quietly at first and then louder so that people next to him stop their hugging to look over.

I lift my wings and engulf him. I spot Chick rushing over from the other side of the room. I squeeze even harder.

His legs start to do this vibrating thing that looks like an odd jig. He wiggles his shoulders, trying to shake me off, but I am unflappable. I plant my feet on the ground and tighten.

"I think you're hurting him," Monkey notes.

Chick is at my side, trying to pry a wing between my father and me, but she lacks the strength to wedge us apart. She tries to push her wing deeper, the friction causing yellow feathers to rise above us.

Why is she getting involved?

Dad is now making a gurgling sound.

Everyone's yelling things at me, but their words blur together into one inaudible buzz.

Mikey runs over and starts blowing his whistle. I squeeze harder.

"Abort, Cuddler 82. Abort immediately!"

A few participants try to pull my arms away, but that only makes me grip harder.

My fingers are cramping. I only want to focus on the strength of my squeeze.

Chick kicks me hard in the shins again and again until I can't hold on any longer.

The next thing I know Dad is on the floor. Someone brings him water. Mikey is apologizing profusely. Monkey and Bunny have their fuzzy paws on my chest in case I decide to stage another attack.

Chick is nowhere to be seen.

Dad doesn't press charges, but I'm still fired on the spot. The Cuddle Party ends early. Guests are shaken. As I'm escorted out in full costume, I hear Dad muttering to Mikey, "Your goddamn turkey."

I don't bother changing before I get home. Sure, the costume belongs to the Cuddle Corporation, but they won't ask for it back. No one is ever going to want to cuddle with a turkey again.

It's raining, and there's nothing on this bird to wick the water away. It just gathers in damp clusters, weighing me down.

I had a good thing going with this cuddling business. I was the best of the best.

The army won't be so bad. There are critters there too. Monkeys at least. Smart monkeys. Clever monkeys.

The street is hazy with damp fog, and the streetlamps shine blurry halos of light. As I make my way to the base of the tree, yellow feathers float past me to the ground. I look up.

"Chick?"

She looks down at me, stooped over a branch of the ash. *Chick?*

"Shh! You'll wake Mom!" She waves me away but loses her footing and slips down the rain-slickened trunk, landing on the grass on her butt.

"Your feathers are falling off." I say to my sister while passing her a yellow clump.

"That's the least of our problems."

# Roadkill

––––––

They won't give her a bra. Or underwear. Or lipstick.

She is slowly being erased.

"You gonna let me fuck you tonight?"

*Kind of him to ask*, Jaime thinks, even though it's a rhetorical question.

Her small cell is shared with Joe, a behemoth of a cellmate. With tattooed arms and legs and neck and face, he could be the strong man in the circus had he chosen a different career path.

The building is surrounded by five barbed-wire fences, four ID checkpoints, two guard towers, and a fifty-thousand-volt electric fence. A guard explained the ropes when Jaime entered the facility two weeks ago, face still bloodied.

The cuts are crusted over now, replaced by a more subdued color, like Merlot. Or that lipstick, French Love, which Jaime used to save for nights when she wanted to look more sophisticated.

Her mother used to tell her, "In French, your name means 'I love you.'" When men made love to her and called out her name, she translated their breathy voices as saying, *I love you, I love you.* Although they rarely did.

The prison lies halfway between Las Vegas and Los Angeles in a desert where people only ever pass by, always on their way to somewhere more interesting. Nothing but shades of brown. Shit brown. Bile brown. Mucus brown. Dirt brown. In the summer, the heat makes one feel like melting and in the winter, the wind whips through the mountains and gets caught there, volleying back and forth like a heated game of ping-pong.

Jaime refuses to look at herself in the mirror, hasn't seen her own image since she got there. But she can feel her greasy hair slick back on its own. She pictures her wigs lined up on their mannequin heads at home. She named them: Marilyn, Joan, Rita. Sitting proudly like busts of famous composers on a piano.

Since entering prison, her body has started to change, morph into what it once was, what it should never have been. The dark brown hair is sprouting back on her face. Without the hormones, she is becoming angrier. Her voice is descending downward a half note each day. At least she still has her breasts.

"Inmate number 47384902, the doctor will see you now."

The doors of her cage unlock.

Amos straightens his name tag before two guards bring the diminutive man to him. Amos nods at the men who stay just on the other side of the door, peering through the shatterproof-glass window. He rifles through a pile of files and extracts Jaime Rodriguez's.

"You've been waiting a while to see the doctor," says Amos.

"Yes, it is you I've been waiting for." Jaime's left lip turns upward. It verges on flirtation. Amos shakes it off.

"I have a few questions for you. I see you've filed a complaint about your hormones. Were you receiving physician-prescribed hormones before the time of incarceration?" Amos feels comfortable with big words. He has spent over sixteen years reading through the prison library.

"My hormones I received on the black market, from a guy who knew a girl who knew a doctor. So, yes, technically, they came from a real doctor. But I never met him."

"Aha."

Both men notice a cockroach moving across the floor.

"They used to come only at night. But lately, they've been getting brave." Amos's pencil scratches across medical forms like a dancer performing soft-shoe.

He doesn't reveal that he's not a doctor, not even a certified nurse, but rather inmate number 43759218, who's been here long enough to have developed a career cleaning wounds and taking notes and vital signs. He helps Dr. Nobel four times a week and does one shift as a wannabe EMT, riding in ambulances to highway accidents, administering first aid, or sealing up body bags. He had earned everyone's trust, getting rides from an armed guard to the hospital, where he'd sit with real medical professionals, waiting for disaster to strike on the highway.

"Give me your left arm."

Jaime obliges.

"That feels good," says Jaime.

Amos recoils. "I'm trying to find a vein."

"I think I have none."

"They're just not pronounced. Look at mine." Amos pulls up his sleeve to reveal bulging veins the size of telephone cords. "It all depends on what God gives you."

"I have little faith in God. God accidentally gave me a penis."

Amos pierces the skin with a small needle attached to a long, clear tube. The blood flows out and is caught in a vial with a pink rubber seal. Jail is all about fluids going in and out, in and out like the ocean tides.

A third man enters the room wearing a white coat.

"I'm Dr. Nobel. I see you've met Amos, our *helper*."

Amos cringes at the word and hands the doctor Jaime's file. Prison negotiates power. Who has it. Who wants it. What you're willing to do to get it. Amos rubs elbows with medical professionals, but is still locked behind bars at night. He only ever has a few minutes to play doctor before his true status is revealed.

The doctor closes the file and turns to Jaime.

"This is where the problem lies. Because you weren't officially receiving hormones from a doctor, we can't diagnose you with gender identity disorder, and you need that diagnosis in order to receive hormone medication in here."

"But I am not a man."

Amos wants to tell her to stay silent. Complacency will get her everywhere.

"What if I'd had the surgery already?" asks Jaime.

Amos's eyes widen. Was she really a full *she*?

The doctor responds, "Then I'd have no choice but to give you the hormones. Have you had the surgery?"

Jaime shakes her head. "I'll be sure and get that done before my next arrest, I promise."

Amos cracks a half-smile.

The doctor checks Jaime's chart. "Manslaughter is no laughing matter." He puts the folder back in the pile, a signal to the guards on the other side of the window to return.

"Let us know if you need anything." Amos has heard doctors speak using the royal "we."

Because of her good behavior, Jaime is allowed to join the prison work force. She had been selected for the sewing department, her hands a perfect fit for the nimble job of ripping out "Made in Honduras" labels attached to clothing and sewing on labels that read "Made in the U.S.A."

Jaime hopes to run into the man in the blue scrubs with the chiseled features and that cleft in his chin she could get lost in. At night, she self-soothes, reminding herself how Amos had taken her arm before blood was drawn and stroked the area where her ulna met her humerus. Her mother used to do the same thing when she was a child. She had been a nurse and understood the working mechanisms of the body, but not why her child had so many body issues.

At work, Jaime keeps her head down while she works. She doesn't talk to the other men. But they talk to her:

"Bet those hands of yours would work nice down my pants."

"Later, we're gonna get you, pretty boy. You won't be so pretty anymore."

Jaime makes $5.75 an hour, hunched over her sewing machine. But she won't get any earnings until she's released. She is saving up for the operation. She's done the math; she will need to rip 382,000 labels to pay for the surgery. These labels have a freedom she no longer possesses. They will be sewn to shirts and folded on store shelves. They will be fingered by other living human beings. They will have the sun fade their colors while Jaime sits behind bars, rotting. Testosterone gathering in her body like angry drunks on the Vegas strip.

After she gets the surgery, it will take only a week to recover before emerging like a butterfly from a chrysalis. She will reenter the world as Glenda Rodriguez: good witch of the North. She will fall in love with a strong man who will take good care of her and buy her a house with a sturdy dishwasher.

Jaime is jolted out of her reverie when a power ballad blasts over the radio loudspeaker. She looks around. The big bald guy with the dragon tattoo is singing along. Jaime laughs just as this man looks up from his performance. Later, he will come up to Jaime when the foreman steps outside for a smoke and hold a knife to her neck. He will tell her if she ever shows her teeth again he will slit her ear to ear. The next day, Jaime's hands will tremble so badly, she will find it nearly impossible to remove any "Made in Honduras" labels for the first hour.

"They got you pretty bad."

Amos stitches up Jaime's left eye and then rubs alcohol on it. He dabs an elongated cotton swab across the swollen, bloodied and blue flesh.

"It is just skin. It will heal," says Jaime. "That guard, by the door. He was there when I was first admitted. He ordered a strip search."

"Protocol," says Amos. "To check for drugs and weapons. Contraband."

"I was naked. His eyes lingered. I was holding red heels. And a lipstick called French Love."

"You have nice hands," Amos hears himself say without thinking. He could lose his position if he blurs the lines between patient and *helper*. But being close to his release date gives him confidence.

Jaime turns her palms downward and examines her own hands as though for the first time.

"My mother always wanted for me to learn the piano."

"Did you?"

"Where would I practice? I did not know anyone who owned a piano."

Two cockroaches turn dizzily in circles, making faint clicking noises as though trying to locate one another on the floor.

"They look confused," says Jaime.

"It's the Cypermethrin. They're putting it through the vents to kill the bugs. It makes them disoriented."

The cockroaches stumble.

"I have something for you," says Amos. "But you gotta be cool. Those guards might be watching, so just stay where you are. I'm going to bend down like I dropped something. You do the same and I'll give it to you that way." His chest pounds as he leans forward and his cheek, washed in stubble, brushes across Jaime's. "Now," he mouths and flashes a piece of red fabric through the cuff of his sleeve, which Jaime grabs and tucks into her own cuff before they both sit up straight and glance toward the guards who are distracted, talking to one another.

"We have our own black market here. Stuff isn't easy to come by. But I saw these and thought of you. Let me know if you like them."

"When can I see you again?" asks Jaime.

Before Amos answers, the doctor comes in to check on his work.

"Who did this to you?" the doctor asks. Amos knows the victim never speaks out or else the next time will be ten times worse. He looks at the linoleum floor where he counts the drops of blood that have fallen from Jaime's face.

"I'm ordering an administrative segregation."

"What does this mean?" asks Jaime.

The doctor explains, "No work. No recreation. You'll basically be in isolation until this passes. It's for your own protection."

Jaime makes a feeble sound of protest.

"It's that, or I could reassign you to a psychiatric prison."

"There's nothing wrong with my mind," says Jaime.

Amos wipes the blood from the floor with a rag.

"Of course not," says the doctor, condescendingly. "I'm just letting you know your options."

"Segregation, *por favor*," Jaime says, as though she's ordering coffee at the local diner.

The doctor scratches his pen across a page in Jaime's file.

"Come back in a week. Amos will remove those stitches."

Amos peels off the rubber gloves. Barriers lie between workers and prisoners, latex and bodily fluid. But behind bars, in the dark, fluids comingle without apprehension.

The first thing Jaime does in isolation is remove the red fabric from her cuff. It's women's lace underwear. Jaime wonders what else Amos can get. How did he pay for this? She quickly takes off her jumpsuit and boxer briefs and places her ankles through the openings of the panties. After steadying herself, she bends forward and guides the soft fabric over her calves, knees, thighs, until they rest on her square hips, digging slightly into her skin. Jaime takes a moment to revel in the flirtatious lace before stepping into her jumpsuit, proud of the secret concealed underneath.

At first, isolation seems like a spa getaway. She's been segregated her entire life, one way or another. How is this any different? Jaime can sleep at night without worrying about a visit from Joe. She can use the toilet in private. She can dance in her cell without apprehension, singing Dusty Springfield in her head, imagining she is wearing a bright yellow boa around her neck.

But then the loneliness settles in. She wonders if she really would rather be with those monster-like men just for the sake of some company. The guards come and go so quickly: to do a check a few times a day, to drop off food. She tries to lure them to stay longer by asking easy questions,

"What's the weather like outside?"

"What's going on in the news?"

But they don't bite.

The doctor said he'll keep her there until *this passes*. But how can he quantify desire?

Even the bugs and rodents steer clear of isolation.

For one hour, once a day she's taken out to "the yard," a twenty-by-ten-foot plot of concrete where she can see for herself what the weather is like. Excruciating heat. Well over one hundred degrees. It makes her sweat and pustules form on her face and back. What she wouldn't give for an exfoliating bath. Everything that touches her skin in prison is harsh and calloused. Softness doesn't exist here. Even the mashed potatoes are grainy. She suns herself, like a dog.

The only other time she's allowed to leave is to take a shower, every other day. A guard escorts her down the halls to the main prison, where she is led past men who spit and jeer. She removes the underwear and hides it in her bed sheets. One misstep could cost her her life.

Today, the only free showers are at the back of the room, the light above flickering a few times before going out. Maintenance checks are not a priority here. Jaime doesn't want to see her body anyway—just wants to quickly go through the motions with the soap—"cleaning every crevice" as her mom used to remind her. The water is coarse and smells like minerals.

When she feels someone approach, she keeps her head down, resigned to her fate, too tired to fight. But it's Amos who takes Jaime's head and gently turns it toward him. Amos moves closer until his flesh is against Jaime's wet skin, quickly arousing them. In this moment, Jaime doesn't care if she's caught. In this moment, she doesn't care if her throat is slit by a jealous onlooker. Nothing is more worth it.

Amos reaches his hand down between Jaime's legs. Jaime doesn't want him to feel her erect penis, this member she's not supposed to have. She guides Amos's hands instead up to her own breasts, nipples erect. Amos makes a faint moaning sound. Jaime catches a glimpse of the moldy grout in the tiles and then looks at the floor where a drowned cockroach is caught in a counterclockwise undertow of the shower's draining system, spinning like a cyclone.

Back in isolation, Jaime will begin to refuse first food and then water. After six days the door will finally unlatch and she will be taken to the prison clinic. Amos will no longer work there. He will have been released after sixteen years behind bars because he's served his time for shoplifting a six-pack of beer, his third strike in a string of more serious crimes: grand theft auto. Battery. A new helper will hook Jaime up to bags of clear fluid. This attendee will have trouble locating a vein and leave her bruised and blue, a color her body is getting used to. This new attendee won't talk to her, he'll just watch as the bag empties into her body. And Jaime will picture Amos waiting for her outside the prison gates.

They had been bored when they got the call, cruising the stretch of highway that spanned between Ghost Town and Pahrump. The driver flipped the switch, sending the lights atop the ambulance into a dizzy swirl of red and white as the deafening siren sounded. Amos, sitting in the back with the equipment, where prisoner volunteers had to stay, braced himself.

It was a seven-car collision. Witnesses later said they had seen a red car veering in and out of lanes. Most likely a drunk driver. It took a while for enough help to arrive. A medicopter was called: it would eventually land in the desert, whipping up its own wind over spiny succulents. People on their way to Las Vegas would complain about the bumper-to-bumper traffic keeping them from their big jackpot, and tourists on their way home, broke and hung over, would wish they never had taken the trip.

"Next time, we'll fly," many would say.

Two medics unlocked the latch and released Amos from the back of the ambulance, flares in hand. Then the driver and the medic sitting in the passenger seat followed. They separated, approaching three different crashed cars. The other four automobiles would have to wait for more help to arrive. Amos activated the flares and placed them diagonally across the road, reducing the highway's four lanes to just one. When there were enough medics to help, his job would be traffic controller, waving cars forward, keeping lookie-loos from halting the flow of traffic.

Amos was sent to check on the red Corolla. Before he reached the car he stared out into the dark, open desert. He could use this moment, these other people's misfortunes, as an opportunity to disappear. Refuse to do his last few months. But the sight of the car halfway down an embankment, hood bent in angular directions, like a larger version of a recycled soda can crushed by bare hands, reminded him he was needed here.

Shining a light into the car, he saw there was only one victim. A woman, slumped over the steering wheel. Carefully, Amos pried open the door. Up ahead, he could hear the clanking metal of the the Jaws of Life being used to remove a body or two from an overturned car down the road.

"Ma'am, I'm here to help." He was met with silence. He snapped the latex gloves out of his back pants pocket and put them on. He wasn't authorized to lift bodies, but this seemed like a do-or-die situation. As he shifted the woman, he heard the rattle of glass. A bottle of vodka rolled onto the carpeted floor of the car. A red high heel was missing. She still had a pulse, and he gently moved her so that her back rested on the seat. The woman's auburn hair cascaded over her shoulders. Her face was bloodied, clashing with the color of her bright lipstick.

Amos removed the small plastic barrier from his pocket, used to help administer CPR without allowing any germs to cross over into his own mouth. He breathed life into the woman and watched as her chest rose while he silently counted—her breasts rising and then falling.

Amos drowned out the shouts from outside and focused only on breath in, one-one hundred, two-one-hundred, three-one-hundred, and then the involuntary exhale.

Once she could breathe on her own, he picked up her purse from the floor on the passenger's side, hoping to find some form of identification or any medical information he should know about. He rifled through makeup and square packaging containing condoms until he came across her wallet. He removed a plastic card that showed not a woman but a slight and serious-looking man, Esteban Jaime Rodriguez.

He wondered how Mr. Rodriguez would react to his wife's accident. *Where was she going alone so late at night? Why had she been drinking?* Luckily he wouldn't have to be the one to inform him.

"That an open bottle?"

More EMTs had arrived on the scene.

"Better get the cops on this one. Don't touch anything. Except the lady."

"Can I get a stretcher over here?" Two medics scurried forward and helped Amos transfer the woman with torn fishnets to the metal platform. In Roman times, emperors rode around on essentially the same mechanism.

Police investigated the crime scene. She was the only one with open containers of alcohol in her vehicle. When she became stable, she would blow air into a breathalyzer and come up with a blood count of .10 percent. She would be read her rights and taken to the women's prison facility eighty miles away. But the next day she would be transferred to the men's.

Amos restocked the used linens in the ambulance. He cleaned his CPR aid with disinfectant. He checked the levels of oxygen in the tanks and wrote the date, in pencil, on a green card hanging off the tank nozzle. He was happy to take a break from vertical bars.

Body bags passed him and were put into adjacent medical vehicles.

On the ride home he morphed back into a prisoner. Only the landscape stayed consistent. People were ever-changing. He looked out the window at the surrounding mountains—like a "sleeping lady," the EMTs would always say. But Amos only ever saw a man, calloused and tired, broken and worn.

# Airborne

———

"Pregnant or fat?"

It's a game you play when you're stuck having to watch people, say, file into a theater or, in this case, board an airplane.

Sitting in first class already has its drawbacks and you haven't even taken flight yet. All that money for a few inches of extra leg room and pre-boarding just means you get to sit the longest, forced to watch the unattractive mishmash of Americans and Germans file past.

"Pregnant or fat?" Let the games begin.

The first two women are definitely just fat. Their bodies barely fit the aisle. Hip lard bumps your left shoulder as one makes her way to her seat. Their fat sits everywhere—arms, calves, double chins. The third dumpy damsel could be pregnant. She's mostly proportionate, apart from the bulging belly. You have to work hard not to ask when she's due.

*Stop it. Be nice.* You sort of believe in karma. Grandma Sue used to give money to airport solicitors, thinking her charity would keep the plane in the sky. Grandma Sue was a benevolent idiot.

Pat Mountain promised a sunny day on the morning show, but you've brought provisions just in case he got it wrong: six small bottles of vodka purchased in duty-free and one bottle of Xanax. If there's one perk in the benign life of a pharmaceutical sales representative, it's getting to sleep with the doctors who will write you prescriptions for anything.

The pilots had already boarded by the time you made it to the gate, which means you didn't get to introduce yourself to them ahead of time, or announce your fears and make sure they looked alert and sober.

Pretending to be brave and optimistic, you memorize the various recline button angles, so you'll be able to adjust the seat while wearing your eye mask.

Why is that dark-skinned, dark-haired man so unhappy? Is it because he is about to hijack this plane and he knows these are his last moments of life? His cargo pants have a suspicious number of pockets. Security couldn't possibly have checked them all. Where are the strapping, fair-skinned, pleasant-looking men who can be sure to help out when Mr. Unhappy makes his move? You twist to peer into economy and note a few more suspects.

Harsha would be useless in any in-flight hijacking situation. He's too small for heroics. You borrowed a shirt of his when you were cold one night after making love—it fit perfectly.

"Why do you have women's clothing?" you asked accusingly.

"Sometimes I prefer the women's cut. It hugs my frame better." It's just the whacked-out thing he would do. Like that pair of pink jeans. Or his leopard-print RV seats.

A woman stops at your row and climbs over you to seat 12A. She is definitely both pregnant and fat.

"I'm Amy," she says, before sitting down beside you.

You reluctantly nod. This is not an office mixer.

"First class was a gift to *us* from my husband." She pats her belly, waiting for you to acknowledge her breeding prowess. Some people believe it means you're less likely to crash if kids or pregnant women are on board; maybe you should be thankful, but instead you focus on how Amy Jr. will surely inherit his mother's annoying gene.

"I don't even mind that we're in the last row of first class because twelve is my lucky number. It's a pretty good lucky number to have. Eggs. Doughnuts. Days of Christmas. It's like good luck is all around me. Charlie thinks I should give the baby twelve names. It's a boy. We like Jonah and Zachary for sure, but can't quite agree on the other ten. What are your favorite boy names?"

"Damien," you say, reaching for a celebrity gossip magazine, hoping it will save you from the chatterbox.

"Champagne? Mimosas?" A cheery flight attendant offers.

"I'm pregnant," Amy practically sings.

A mimosa may make Ms. Diarrhea-of-the-Mouth less annoying.

"Oh my god, it's what's-her-name. This pregnancy makes me all foggy-brained," blurts Amy.

Walking toward you is Jazzy McGhee, the one from that reality show set at a rehab center—actress, singer, model. Her story has been told a thousand times. Got hooked on drugs early, slept her way to the top, lost custody of her children, married, then divorced three celebrities (one actor, one producer, and one late-night infomercial salesman whose claim to fame was his fast-talking enthusiasm for an automatic citrus peeler) and now has cleaned up her act—a poster child for sobriety. You religiously watched every episode, even lied to Harsha about it because you knew he wouldn't approve. He doesn't own a TV; his RV doesn't get satellite.

So there she is, Jazzy McGhee, walking down the aisle like a queen, neither pregnant nor fat. Other passengers' eyes light with recognition and they begin to whisper. She takes a seat across the aisle from you. Amy waves at her like they've been lifelong friends. A male flight attendant rushes to Jazzy's side, takes her bag, and places it in the overhead compartment. You didn't get the same treatment. The other bag she keeps at her feet. The other bag is moving. And whimpering. The flight attendant leans down to inspect it.

"How cute!" he exclaims.

Great. You wait for the sneezing and wheezing to begin.

Harsha had a pit bull you hated. Derrida. Eighty-five pounds of unpredictable hard-packed flesh. She had been a professional fighting dog in South Central. Then the police busted the illegal ring; she was taken to the pound, where Harsha saved her just minutes before she was slated to be euthanized. Had to bring a bottle of Benadryl every time you went over there. The only person she liked was Harsha and she growled maniacally every time you knocked on the door of the RV. If Harsha hadn't been there to let you in and Derrida somehow had gotten out, you're sure she would have killed you. In the middle of the night, when you had to pee, she would snarl at your heels all the way to the bathroom. Harsha would sleep right through it and not believe you in the morning.

"She's a doll. She's so thankful for being rescued; she'd never hurt anyone."

Harsha trusted everyone. It was his biggest flaw. Like that time he parked your car when you couldn't find street parking on RV row in Venice Beach.

"Where are my keys?" you asked when he got back (you pumped Derrida full of Milk Bones while he was gone so she wouldn't sic).

"I left them folded in the visor."

"You locked them in the car?"

"I'm not daft. The car is unlocked. They're just there, so we won't lose them."

By the time your shoes were on, the car was gone. You found it three blocks away. A few things missing: a sweater, some CDs, an overpriced lip gloss.

"This isn't the fucking Indian countryside!"

At the police station three men in uniform laughed at you for being with such a loser. They asked for Harsha's address and he said, "Halfway down Rose Avenue, third RV on the left." They laughed even harder. It's there and then you decided it was over. Time to sever all ties. Back to men with appointment books and blank prescription pads. You would spend three month's salary on a first-class ticket to Europe because you'd been slumming it for the past two years. You promised to never set foot in a mobile home ever again.

Everyone on the plane is seated except for Mr. Unhappy, scowl growing as he speaks with a flight attendant in the galley. They should make him sit down. The Xanax isn't working yet and you wish you had taken one two hours ago. Maybe if you take another one, you'll just sleep through the flight. If you could hire an anesthesiologist to pump your veins full of the good stuff, you would. Maybe you should start a business. The slogan would be: Sleep through anything.

The safety video feels like a litany of all the things that could go wrong.

Engines rev and then slow as the plane reverses away from the gate. A flock of ducks has gathered on the runway. You try to mentally shoo them away, reminded of a story you once heard about a bird getting caught in an engine on takeoff, taking the whole plane down.

The dog is now out of its carrier and sitting on Jazzy's lap. It's more of a puppy really, which means it's going to bark and it's probably not potty trained. Your eyes close as the engines rumble during takeoff. Amy is quiet for now, her headphones on, eyes closed, both hands resting on her swollen belly. You squint to look out the window to make sure the plane is still heading in an upward angle, listening carefully for variances in the engine noises. If you're going down, you want to be the first to know.

Cars, houses, and then mountains shrink to dollhouse proportions. Once the plane has leveled, you recall what your flight therapist said, over twenty years ago, when you refused to go with your parents to Hawaii for the holidays.

"It's just like a boat on the water. Planes don't just fall out of the sky."

You reminded him about the *Titanic*, the *Lusitania*, the *General Slocum*. That year you ended up spending Christmas with Mrs. Montague, your aging neighbor, learning how to knit your own stocking, which looked more like an elephant's limp trunk. It hung sadly from her fireplace mantle while your parents sunned themselves, downing mai tais.

When you first met Harsha you felt as though you were being rebellious—dating a "brown man" as he liked to refer to himself. You knew his arms, emblazoned with tattoos (Ganesha, a medieval cross, the Queen of England), would shock your friends and family. This choice was so unlike you. But you also knew that his job as a History of Consciousness professor at UCLA would help counter any misconceptions people had about him.

But you didn't sign on for the RV. Or the pit bull.

"I just don't need all those material things," he explained the first time you went "home" with him for a nightcap.

"Like doorbells and walls?"

He patted you on the head. Derrida growled jealously.

"It's fascinating here. A real sociological study. It's like a modern-day West Side Story with the rivalry between the RV owners and the city of Venice."

You took a leap of faith and started whistling the Jets' song.

Without skipping a beat Harsha picked right up, "From your first cigarette / to your last dying day."

"Ladies and gentleman, the captain has turned off the seatbelt sign. It is now safe to walk about the cabin. We advise you to please keep your seatbelts fastened when seated in case of any unexpected turbulence."

You automatically tighten your seatbelt and catch Amy's eye; she's making the oddest expression, eyes squinting, lips pursed.

"I'm practicing my kegels. You know, tightening the muscles of my pelvic floor. It'll make it so that my bladder doesn't get weak after childbirth. Helps during pregnancy too . . . I was having some accidents when I sneezed. It's been a lot better since doing these exercises. You should try them! You don't have to be pregnant for them to work. Do you have kids?"

"I'm not really a big talker on planes."

Amy wilts in her seat and places her hands on her belly. She assumes the fetus likes her.

Up ahead, Mr. Unhappy is fidgeting, looking all around him like a curious pigeon on a stoop.

"Flying is safer than driving!" Harsha used to remind you when you had to travel back east to visit relatives. His father is still in London, his mother in India. He is no stranger to transatlantic flights. You'd have made the six-day drive to Pennsylvania in a heartbeat if your job had allowed more time off. Besides, in a car there's only a matter of inches between you and the pavement. How could he not get that?

The only time you flew together was to Las Vegas, on your company's dime, for a pharmaceutical sales conference. Harsha fell asleep before the plane took off. He refused to wake up, even after you poked him with your drink stirrer. Hard.

"It's just what happens when I get on planes," he pleaded after the rocky landing had you swearing you'd never cheat on him again if you survived.

"Fuck you," you said when the rubber tires finally met asphalt.

Nothing seemed to faze him. Life was in his control or at least he seemed to float along freely through it. How was it that he never got angry? What did the voices inside his head sound like? Nothing like the bitter chatter echoing inside yours. You fight to remember the things in between the drama: the underside of the stool in his RV kitchen where he stuck his chewed-up gum.

"It's a sculpture," he said. "What Michelangelo could have done with a pack of gum." Then he shared with you the meaning of "chiaroscuro" and turned the spelling of the word into a drinking game that included one tequila shot for every misspelling. You were drunk at the first "o."

Then there was the time you walked down Abbot-Kinney and caught him getting a pedicure. You stood at the window of the salon for at least five minutes before he looked up, noticed you, and waved. You felt as though you had caught him masturbating. But he was nonplussed. You fell in love with him because he didn't play by the rules. And you fell apart because you failed to play by his.

"In a few moments, we will begin dinner service for first-class passengers. Your choices this evening are chicken piccata, salmon bake, or eggplant Parmesan."

The Xanax and mimosa combination take over and you fall into a surprisingly deep sleep, momentarily awakened by what you think is screaming. Which ends up just being laughter.

At least four hours must have passed. Maybe more. Your body is stiff from staying in the same position for so long. It's okay you've slept through dinner because at least a third of the flight is over. But according to your watch, somehow incredibly, only two minutes have passed since you shut your eyes. Jazzy's dog is looking at you, like she knows what you're thinking. Do animals even make the victims list when planes crash?

Time for another Xanax. This time you crush it with a plastic spoon and drop the white powder into whatever is left of your mimosa. It's the fast-acting approach that takes you to your happy place. If someone looked over at you, they'd think you were a calm flyer.

Amy is taking a German lesson on the monitor in front of her.

"Mein name ist Amy," she says, unaware of how loudly she's speaking. Tapping her on the shoulder, you bring your forefinger to your lips.

"Ich bin Amerikaner," she whispers.

Before you know it, you're finally fast asleep, for real this time, hovering thirty thousand feet above the ultra-abyssal zone, yet another geographical site you know little about.

You dream about the men you may meet in a new country. They will smell of cigarettes and beer. There will be miscommunications, which can be to your benefit. No one knows the real you, allowing you to be whomever you want to be. You can have flings and sleep until noon. You can meet a rugged German who has a knee-licking fetish. You will make sure your legs are always shaved for him. Or not.

When you wake up, Jazzy's dog is incessantly licking your knee.

"Come here, Puffin." The dog farts by your side before returning to her owner.

"Sorry about that. She's just very affectionate."

You're not impressed with celebrity, at least not this kind, and muster a fake smile. Jazzy seems too needy. The way she was too afraid to sleep alone as contestants were eliminated and she insisted on bunking with the teen heartthrob. If you start up a conversation now, you'll be stuck listening to her for at least five more hours. Instead, you take a napkin and wipe the slobber off your knee. Puffin hops onto Jazzy's lap. The flight attendant comes rushing over. He will surely insist that the dog needs to stay in the carrying case.

"I brought her some water." He hands Jazzy a plastic cup.

"How thoughtful."

The flight attendant's rear end is in your face as he bends down to pet the dog. What would he do if you quickly poked your finger up his butt? Would you get slapped with an FCC violation?

"Your show has really inspired me," he begins.

Jazzy takes his hand.

He starts to cry. "I've been sober five years. The hardest years of my life. But the happiest."

You're trapped in a real-life episode of *Oprah*.

"Oh my god! It's really kicking up a storm!" Before you can stop her, Amy grabs your hand and places it on her belly. There are frantic movements and sharp kicks like even the kid wants to escape this woman.

"Isn't that incredible?" says Amy.

"It's disgusting." It's better to tell the truth before she makes anyone else feel her. "I have to pee."

Walking up the aisle, you're still a little shaky from the Xanax. There's a short line. The headrest of the seat in front steadies you. Which part of your body would hit first if you were catapulted to the top of the fuselage? A mousy flight attendant brings three trays of food into the cockpit. When the door cracks open, you catch a glimpse of the back of the heads of the three men in charge of your life. A small trickle of urine releases and drips down your thigh. You squeeze your pelvic floor tight, attempting a kegel.

Mr. Unhappy makes it to the bathroom first and you stand there listening for suspicious sounds. Why are there locks on bathroom stalls six miles high? It's just not safe. You know how long it takes to do one's business and when he exceeds the allotted time limit, you're compelled to notify the flight attendant, sure that he's in there lighting a shoe bomb, tie bomb, penile shaft bomb.

The attendant serving your first-class section is still pouring his heart out to Jazzy. You grab another attendant as she walks by, a breezy, fresh-faced girl who probably goes home with hotshots on her layovers.

"Excuse me."

You search for the right words to accuse Mr. Unhappy of foul play. Just then, the lock on the lavatory clicks and he emerges, his abundant hair slicked back. His hands damp from washing.

"Yes?" smiles the attendant.

"Can I ask you something?"

"Sure."

"What happens if someone dies on board? I mean, has that ever happened?" Maybe your voice is too loud. People around you are staring. The rest seem to have received a memo that it's naptime.

"It has happened," says the flight attendant in a hushed tone. "More than once."

"And?"

"We don't have many options. We try to make them look peaceful. Cover them with a blanket until we land."

Sleeping passengers lie under matching navy blue blankets. Any of them could be dead. All suffocated by noxious gas.

In the bathroom, you snoop for a hidden bomb. But it really doesn't make a difference whether you're sitting right on the bomb or at the back of the plane—in either case, you're going down. Better to have empty bowels and bladder.

As luck would have it, the second you make contact with the paper seat cover the plane begins to jerk. Why has no one thought to install seatbelts in airplane bathrooms? Your regular coping mechanism is singing show tunes. This time it's a shaky rendition of "Guys and Dolls." It's a method that has helped you through one serious car accident and many California earthquakes. Someone bangs on the door. You sing louder until the shaking stops. As you let go of the damp sink, you're reminded of Harsha's attempt at playing therapist the day before a flight you had been dreading.

"What do you hate about it?" he asked.

"I don't know. The lack of control."

"When else in life do you lack control?"

"Everywhere. The DMV. The hairdresser."

"What about while making love?" he asked.

"I don't want to talk about this," you said. Harsha dipped his finger into the peanut butter jar and offered it to Derrida. You looked forward to that night's secret date with a lawyer just because you could get away with it.

Mr. Unhappy creepily stares at you stumbling back to your seat. Jazzy and the flight attendant are clutching hands and crying. You are feeling woozy. Time for one last Xanax.

The flight attendant is holding a disposable camera. "Oh, would you mind taking a picture of us?" He leans in toward Jazzy and they both smile.

You purposely aim the camera just a hint to the left so that all this steward will see when he develops the film is his own face.

It's time to break out the big guns. When your duty-free mini vodka bottles clink together, Jazzy looks over in a Pavlovian reaction. You smile, open one, and swig. Jazzy mumbles something.

"What?" you ask. Jazzy pats the empty seat next to her, inviting you over.

"How many more of those do you have?" she whispers.

"Enough. Want one?" What do you care if Jazzy falls off the wagon? Maybe she never fully hoisted herself onto it in the first place. Maybe the sobriety was all a TV-ratings stunt.

You move to the seat next to her.

"Under the blanket," she says and slips both hands under her blue blanket. You subtly remove a bottle and slide it under until your hands meet. She gives your fingers a squeeze before taking the bottle, her acrylic nails digging into your tender palm. The man across the aisle glares at you.

You stay next to Jazzy because Amy has whipped out a baby-naming book and is quietly arranging names on a piece of paper in sets of twelve and saying them out loud. Adjusting the eye mask on your face and shoving the pink earplugs into your ears, you settle down, hoping to sleep again.

"Ladies and gentleman, the pilot has cordially invited you to a private visit in the cockpit."

As a girl, your mother always brought you to see the pilots. That was *before*. Standing up, you make your way past the bathroom to the open door.

"We've been waiting for you," the elderly pilot says.

"Have a seat," says the copilot, motioning toward the third in command's lap. He straps the belt around the two of you.

The pilot resembles Gumby, verdant and sinewy.

"Enjoying the flight?" asks the copilot, who has a mouthful of gold teeth.

"Oh no, Captain," yells the man whose lap you are occupying. "Duck!!"

Placing your hands protectively over your head, you try to crouch low into his lap. You hear a thud and open one eye. The remnants of a duck are splayed across the windshield.

Someone is shaking your arm.

"Have to talk to the captain," is all you can say.

"The cockpit is closed to visitors, ma'am. You were talking in your sleep. You're making passengers uneasy."

Up a few rows, Mr. Unhappy has turned around, scowling at you.

"I think that man is very suspicious, stewardess," you say, finger pointed toward Mr. Unhappy.

"Ma'am, the only person I'm worried about right now is you."

"They don't call them stewardesses anymore. It's flight attendant." Amy is suddenly their representative.

"But the captain wants me to sit on his lap."

"I'm going to have to ask you to keep it down," demands the *flight attendant*.

"Cockpit," you say, with an emphasis on the first syllable. "*Cock*pit. *Cock*pit. *Cock*pit."

Jazzy is crying. The attendant she was bonding with is stroking her hand. She glares at you.

"What's your problem?" you slur.

The woman seated in front of you turns around in her seat. "You gave da alcoholic der drunk. You should go der hall."

"Deck the halls?" You laugh alone.

"She said 'Go to hell!'" adds her travel companion in a thick German accent.

A few people in first class applaud. If you could just talk to the captain, things would be straightened out. He's on your side. The seatbelt clicks and you stumble toward the front of the plane.

"Where do you think you're going?" the giddy Jazzy fan asks.

"Toseecapin."

"Ma'am, I need you to sit down."

Ignoring her, you grab your cell phone from your fleece pocket. Harsha would know exactly what to say to this *flight attendant* to get you in to see the captain. You begin punching in his number, surprised in a pleasant way, that you want to share your frustration with him. Mr. Happy is next to you grabbing the phone right out of your hand just after you press "Talk." Passengers gasp.

"Terrorist!!" you shout. He forcibly holds your hands behind your back.

"I'm not a terrorist, ma'am. I'm an undercover armed guard, hired to make these skies safer. I'm going to take you back to your seat now." He's pushing you hard in the center of your back. He says to Amy,

"Ma'am, I'm gonna have to ask you to move up a few rows for the rest of the flight."

"But twelve is my lucky number!" Amy shakily gathers her things.

At your seat Mr. Unhappy handcuffs you to his wrist.

Passengers are facing forward again and only sporadically looking back at you to make sure you're still subdued.

"We're like Siamese twins!" you laugh, holding up your arm and his wrist in tandem. No one laughs with you.

"Ladies and gentleman, please place your seats in their full upright position. We will soon begin our descent into Berlin."

Your cell phone begins to blare a familiar ringtone: "I like to be in America. Okay by me in America." The officer picks up the phone. Passengers panic at the way he's scrutinizing it. Using your free hand, you reach over and press the talk button before he has a chance to stop you.

"Harsha? It's me!" You just need to hear his voice, but all you can hear is Derrida barking, muffling out Harsha before your captor ends the call and cuffs your other hand to the seat.

Amy is up ahead complaining of stomach cramps, Jazzy is crossing herself, and when a passenger sneezes, you finally get to hear the correct pronunciation of "Gesundheit." A video tutorial plays explaining the German customs process. You won't get that far.

Out the window the city emerges through the clouds.

The plane lands with a jerky thud. You must stay in your seat until every last passenger exits the aircraft, which gives you ample opportunities to play "Lesbian or cancer?" as women with short hair file past.

# Big Brother

---

We hate Les Kunkel.

We hate the way he flounces around the post office, always with that stupid smile on his face. We hate how the sign next to the box of doughnuts always says, "Brought to you by Les." He never even bothers to get the plain glazed kind, which everyone likes, but tries to impress us with flavors like "raspberry swirl" and "mojito mania."

We hate the way he has to be the first to volunteer to open things when they're stuck: the latch on the Xerox machine, the door to the supply closet that jams, the tab of the tomato juice that Gina, the window clerk, brings with her every day.

We hate that he's been working here for only two months and Gloria, our site manager, has already given him three commendations.

We especially hate that he's missing more than half of his middle finger on his right hand and makes no effort to hide it in his pocket or behind his back when we talk to him, forcing us all to stare at it like we're the ones with the problem.

Kennedy's not at her station when I get to work. Typical. Can't believe they haven't fired her yet. The desk next to hers is also empty; Sarah got pregnant and retired at twenty-three. Gloria still hasn't filled the position.

"Soup for breakfast?"

Levi is sitting at his machine, slurping. He looks up and nods, "Yes, Ernest."

I point to the laminated sign on the wall that read, "No Food Allowed."

Levi brings the plastic bowl to his mouth and tilts it, finishing the last of the soup. He snaps on the lid and places the bowl in a brown lunch bag. I've been working as a postal service clerk for twenty-five years now, since I was twenty-four; people respect me around here.

Can't do as much of the heavy lifting anymore—my back strength isn't what it used to be. And the job's changed a bit now that they have all these new machines. We used to do everything by hand, inputting numbers, addresses, and names. One person was in charge of zip codes. Now, we stick the envelopes into the Multi-line Optical Character Reader, which does all the scanning on its own and even sprays a barcode on the envelope.

But machines, like humans, are prone to bad days and about 10 percent of the mail doesn't get read correctly. Those envelopes come to me, and I look them over and enter the addresses into my computer, which prints out a barcode I have to manually stick to the envelope. Without me, these letters would never get to their intended recipients.

Kennedy strolls in thirty minutes late, earphones on, tattoos exposed.

"I thought we talked about covering up?" I say.

She doesn't respond. How am I supposed to concentrate with the gargoyle on her arm leering at me?

"The tattoo, Kennedy?"

"Oh, Ernest, that's only a rule for the window clerks because they deal with the public," Kennedy says and looks up at Levi.

Since when did they become chummy?

Our heads turn when we hear the mail-truck engines rev. Hurrying to the window, we watch the drivers as they head off on their rounds, marveling at the perfection of their synchronized exit. Must be nice to have all that freedom. When the last truck has left the parking lot, I take a seat and get to work on my pile of machine-rejected letters.

According to the wall clock, we have almost seven hours until we all have to see Les at the weekly staff meeting.

Luckily, I arrive at the pre-meeting late enough that Les has already taken a seat and I plant myself all the way across the room from him. Gloria's got a way of stretching these meetings out with pre-meetings, post-meetings, and sub-meetings—compartmentalizing and labeling until our memo cubbies overflow with color-coordinated handouts.

Crystal Falls is a small operation—a "cozy" post office—and we can all cram into the conference room. We're seated around two fold-up tables, which form a T, and people are digging into a box of assorted doughnuts—limoncello, rosemary, and maple bacon—that Les clearly bought so we'd like him. It's not working. At three o'clock sharp, Gloria hoists herself off her metal chair and taps the table with a plastic comb, calling the meeting to order.

"Thanks for coming, everyone. Edie's taking minutes today. Just a reminder to iron your uniforms; some of you have been looking a bit disheveled. We're representing *the man* here, so we always need to be looking our best. And please take only one cup of coffee in the morning; our budget isn't big enough to support everyone's caffeine habit."

Gloria spits when she talks.

"In other news I've decided to launch a Big Brother program, starting today."

"Why isn't it called a Big Sister Program?" Kimberly, the passport photo operator who's never traveled anywhere, considers herself a feminist.

"You can call it whatever you want. Point is it's starting now. I've matched you all up, oldies with newbies. You're either a mentor or a mentee, and I want you to take this seriously."

Gloria had also organized the Shoes for Africa program where she solicited us all to donate our used shoes. It was a ludicrous endeavor, especially since Gloria kept nagging me about my lack of participation.

"Isn't it *voluntary*?" I kept reminding her. Of course I was right, but the real reason I wasn't participating was that I owned only two pairs myself—work shoes and home shoes—and even the taking-Rufus-for-a-walk sneakers were worn to the point where one had a small hole in the toe of the canvas. Since I was put in charge of placing all the donated shoes into big boxes filled with popcorn packaging and shipping them off to Djibouti, I had first dibs. I picked out two pairs of newer-looking black sneakers, and placed my worn ones in the box with all the other shoes and wished them bon voyage.

"I don't get it," says Terri, who doesn't get much, which is why he's the stamp restocker.

"Follow me," says Gloria, getting up from her chair.

This better not last long. Have to get home to my dog. Gloria leads us all out into the hallway between the sorting room and the front of the post office. She pulls down a huge sheet of butcher paper taped to the wall to reveal another piece of paper where photos of our heads are stuck to paper cutouts of stick-figure bodies. Our elongated hands reach out to our new "sibling." I quickly scan the board and find myself somewhere in the middle, long green arm outstretched to my left, hand stapled onto Les Kunkel's purple one, like we've been crucified together.

"So Big Bro."

It's an annoying thing for Les to say to me because I'm a hell of a lot shorter than him, and it's just like him to bring the obvious to everyone's attention.

"Looks like you're stuck with me. Or should I say stuck to me."

Everyone around us starts laughing, but they're only doing it to make a new guy feel welcome—pump him with confidence. People are standing with their partners, shaking hands, slapping backs. Kennedy is actually hugging Reina.

After our field trip down the hall, Gloria makes us sit down in the meeting room again.

"We have a serious matter to discuss."

Last year Josh, who had been doing delivery rounds for over thirty years, dropped dead of a heart attack on the Pattersons' lawn. That news was announced at a similar meeting. So I assume that someone else has bit the big one.

"We're having an issue with mail going missing," Gloria says. "This makes us look bad. Our job is to get the mail delivered, not lose it. We don't want people to start going to other post offices or, god forbid, use one of those private companies. 'Cause if that's the case, we may as well hang our hats and call it a day."

"We don't wear hats," reminds Terri.

Gloria just scratches the back of her head with her comb.

I thought she was going to go into a whole rant about the glory days of the pony express, but instead she reminds us that it's five years in jail for stealing the mail. We already knew that.

We all start looking around at one another, like how is this mail theft our problem?

Steve's the first one to talk, making himself look suspicious. "That could really mess with a person. Like if you had bills to pay, money due. Creditors would be at your door."

Gloria puts the comb down. "The weird thing is it's all been strictly personal correspondence. Most recently, Greg Garrison's apology to his dying grandmother. She passed and he found out she never received the letter. Could you imagine the guilt that man must feel?"

People nod. Gina makes a clucking sound with her tongue.

"Do any of us really look like the kind of people who steal mail?" I ask Gloria.

"We have to look for the good in people," Les hijacks my altruistic philosophy. "But in case we can't find it, I propose we start an anonymous tip box where people can document any suspicious behavior."

People actually applaud. Anyone could have come up with that idea. It's a no-brainer. Edie puts down her pen and the meeting breaks.

After the room empties I linger in the hallway staring at my purple paper hand still clutching Les's. Making sure no one is coming, I rip the middle finger off of his green hand. Les is missing a finger, and it's not like I'm the only one who's ever noticed. Gloria should have thought of that. I'm sure he wants to be represented accurately.

We all do.

Mrs. Newman is using orange gardening shears to snip at her roses when I pull into my driveway bordering her front garden. Her face is partly hidden by her large brimmed sun hat, but I know she knows I'm there. You can't miss a car pulling up next to you, even if you are a little bit deaf you'd still feel the vibrations, but she doesn't look up. My car door slams. The key ring jingles, but she just continues placing the cut roses into a basket. I wave anyway and decide she must have Alzheimer's.

Rufus is waiting for me on the other side of the door, his tail wagging. When he was little and heard me coming home, he'd shake so exuberantly his tail would bang against the wall and bleed, painting red streaks with his tail brush. Vera thought it was disgusting, but I told her it was proof of his love and propensity for experimental art.

I always do the "Rufus shakedown" when I get home. It starts with one hand on his skull and then my palm shimmies down his spine where I get both hands going and vigorously work my way toward his tail. His top lip curls up whenever I do this, exposing his fleshy pink gum line. It's a move I made up myself—it's supposed to hit all the major pressure points down the back and relieve any arthritis pain.

The various piles around my place would probably look disorganized to the naked eye, but there's definitely a system involved. I've left most things in cardboard boxes since the split with Vera. I fought damn hard for the dinnerware, which sits in two boxes labeled "Fragile, China," but it's not like people come over for dinner, not like I'd ever invite Mrs. Newman over and be stuck having to sit and listen to her talk about begonias all night. The boxes are well taped and make sturdy coffee tables, side by side on the floor. I came across all these paper plates and plastic cutlery in the storeroom at work, so why would I want to unpack all this bubble-wrapped porcelain, which I'm going to have to clean by hand, when I can have a perfectly nice meal and then throw the whole thing away afterwards? I figure I'm sailing on free time spent not doing dishes.

I rest my mail satchel on one of the china boxes. I'm not really supposed to have an official satchel, but when Dean quit he said, "To hell with it," and gave it to me on his way out. Gloria tried to get me to return it, claiming it was official U.S. Government Property, but I told her that my friend gave it to me and therefore it was mine. "Oh, Ernest," she said, which reminded me of how Vera used to say that, which annoyed me even more.

The *M* of the U.S. Mail lettering has faded and looks like it says "U. S ail," like a bumper sticker urging nautical folk to head out to sea.

Breathing in the smell of the leather, I pull out a white envelope. It was the stamp that got me, must've been made at home or something. They can do that now on the computer, but it costs a lot extra. It's a photo of an older couple. The man has his shirt off and is holding a drink. A lot of details can fit on a small stamp. It looks like the woman was the one who held the camera in front of her; the whole frame is a little lopsided. But it made me smile, this couple, and made me wonder what they would have to talk about.

Stickers grab me. So does writing in all capital letters. And writing that slopes downward, especially to the left. By the age of seven the handwriting you have is the handwriting you're going to end up with for the rest of your life. Sometimes, on address labels, I'll see three faint pencil marks where lines had been for idiots who can't write straight.

Little chunks of last night's pasta sauce flick off the plastic fork that I'm using to open the letter. Rufus is already at my feet, licking up the sauce. You'd think I hadn't fed him in days.

There's a feminine curl to the lettering, I assume written by a woman. It's not exactly cursive, but it is frilly. The paper smells faintly of perfume. Rufus sniffs it too and then lies down at my feet.

*Dear Shelley,*

*Don and I had such a nice time with you at the reunion! I can't believe it's been forty years since high school! Did you ever think we'd get back in touch after all these years? Don says you were the most attractive of my friends there. Can you believe he drank three martinis? He woke up with a wallop of a headache the next morning. I had to drive the four hours home and he spent the rest of the day in bed.*

*We hope you come visit sometime. Don says it's a shame you aren't with anyone right now because then we could make a foursome of it, but I think we'll manage just fine, the three of us. Didn't Kelly Sparks look something awful with that face-lift? I bet it cost her a fortune. Don says she looked so perpetually surprised.*

*Let's not wait another thirty-five years to see one another!*

*Alexandra (and Don)*

I close my eyes and picture the reunion scene, imagining myself as Alexandra, then Don, then Shelley. Each has something different to offer—each a window into a world away from my own.

I return to my living room only after Rufus raised his two front paws on the cushions, trying to heave himself up.

"Thatta boy." I lift his rear legs for him. We wait for the five o'clock news to start.

On Monday there's a black backpack on the desk that was empty just last Friday. They've finally filled the position, which means less work for me. Kennedy walks in, her headphones on. There's a big white bandage on her forearm. She must have taken a spill.

I'm hoping Levi will ask her what happened so I don't have to, but when he walks in, he waves and says he'll be right back; he's going to get some coffee.

"What happened?" I ask.

Kennedy doesn't hear me. Her head bops to the music. I tap her on the shoulder, and she jumps.

"Jesus, Ernest! You scared the shit out of me."

Levi comes back into the room, Styrofoam cup in hand. Behind him is Les, who is supposed to be stacking packages in the back room.

"Look who I found!" says Levi.

Les goes over to the desk with the black backpack, places it on the floor, and has a seat.

"What are you doing?" I'm trying my best to use my calm voice.

"Sitting down to my new job, Big Bro; I've been promoted."

"Isn't that great?" asks Levi. Kennedy takes off her headphones and welcomes Les. She actually welcomes him! There must have been some kind of mistake. Or Gloria's lost her last screw.

Les turns to me. "And I have you to thank. Gloria said she thought it would be great if we could work together, be a second set of eyes for you."

How many eyes do I need? I certainly don't need his unibrowed, bulging ones.

"Well, I better get to work." I start typing in digits.

"What happened to your arm?" Les asks Kennedy.

"Oh, I'm okay thanks, just got a new tattoo."

"What of?" asks Les, as if he cares.

"Here, you can see for yourself." She unpeels the tape from the bandage, lifting it off her arm.

"Wow! That's great!"

I'm not surprised that Les is a pretty good liar. I can't see what the picture is, but I don't want Kennedy to think I'm curious. Levi is out of his seat, looking at the tattoo.

"Hey, Ernest, don't you want to see this? It's pretty amazing."

The three of them look over at me.

"We're on the clock. I don't like to steal from Uncle Sam."

We're supposed to be a united front back here.

We shouldn't be taking kindly to Les interrupting our rhythm.

We have daily work rituals we perform together.

The trucks rev their engines and then Kennedy, Levi, and Les rush to the window. I stay seated and hit the numbers on my keypad and count the hours until the workday is done.

At home Mrs. Newman is picking tomatoes behind two new signs nailed to wooden posts that read "No trespassing" and "If you can read this, you're too close to my lawn." Her poor mailman.

"Your dog got out again," she says, refusing to make eye contact.

"It's okay, Mrs. Newman, he knows where he lives."

She takes her spade, points it at me, and throws it down in the dirt. "That's not the point."

"Then what *is* the point, Mrs. Newman?" She's old so I'm showing her I have respect for the elderly by not calling her by her first name. Besides the fact that I have no clue what her first name is. Probably one of those old people names like Bertha or Muriel or Abigail.

"The point is your dog had an accident on my lawn. He just missed my tomatoes."

My laughter is not contagious.

"You know, Mrs. Newman, people use animal feces as compost; it's what makes plants grow better. Maybe Rufus was just trying to help you grow those tomatoes into stronger tomatoes. Into ones with verve."

"I know what compost is. I use it in my garden. Keep your goddamn dog off my lawn."

Rufus is waiting for me on the doorstep.

"Hi boy! Heard you got out today."

He extends a paw, which I pick up and shake. I lean down close to his floppy ear. "Keep up the good work."

Dinner is a package of instant ramen someone left in the lunchroom. Rufus is on the carpet, twitching through a dream. I hope it's the one where he's attacking Mrs. Newman.

My U.S. Mail bag is full of new letters. Today, while sorting through correspondence, I came across a brown envelope decorated with bright balloon stickers. Kennedy was talking on her cell phone to a friend. Levi was concentrating on getting a smudge off his glasses. And Les had just asked me if I wanted a cup of coffee. I don't even drink coffee, but I said, "Yes" just so I could get him out of the room.

*Dear Perry,*

*Remember the time we floated over wine country in that hot-air balloon and you said you could die right then and there with a glass of Zin in one hand and my tit in the other? Just wanted to let you know I was out there again, last weekend, with a guy who reminds me not at all of you and we decided not to go up in those balloons because they're for stuck-up rich people. There was a snake in one of the vineyards. I think I peed myself, which reminded me of how you used to make me laugh. Anyway, hope all is well with you and your mother. You really got to get out of that house if you want to survive.*

*Love,*

*Tina*

My world widens. Hot-air balloons. Wine country.

I picture Tina in purple lingerie, drunk one night, missing Perry, wanting him back but not enough to really do something about it. Letter writing is funny that way; you can be confrontational without ever really having to be brave, like when Vera served me with divorce papers care of the U.S. Mail. "Coward," I wrote back and sent them to her lawyer.

Anyone can read published correspondence between two people: Ernest Hemingway and Georgia O'Keefe. Albert Einstein and FDR. But these letters are better. These letters are all mine.

Rufus is making a faint groaning sound. I lift him up—he gets extra stiff at night—and carry him down the hallway to my bed and place him up by my pillow. His arthritis seems to be getting worse by the day. He's on some real good meds, though, and I can see that they're working. Problem is the meds are so powerful that they'll eventually kill him before the arthritis ever does.

Looking out the kitchen window, I notice Mrs. Newman is sitting around a table with two men and three women. The man at the head of the table says something and everyone erupts in laughter. If only I could read lips. Mrs. Newman gets up from her seat and clears some dishes away. Another woman helps her and when she returns, she's carrying a two-tiered cake on some fancy tray. Her guests seem impressed. It's a real pretty cake.

In front of the post office, old Bruce stands in a torn green t-shirt and shoes with the rubber soles ripped off. He's holding a paper coffee cup in front of him, soliciting change from post-office patrons. I've told Bruce to hit the road before. In fact, I make it a point to do so every chance I get. Have to keep the entrance welcoming if we want customers to keep coming. A bigger post office opened up a couple of years ago, less than two miles from here, with fancy stamp machines and a computerized passport booth. People are easily seduced by that sort of thing. Between that place and the Internet taking over the world, it's surprising we haven't been totally run into the ground.

Bruce sports a small American flag pin on his shirt and tells stories about how he fought in the Gulf War and brags that he's blind in one eye. All these stories for a nickel. You'd think it was hardly worth it. Old ladies with handbags believe him and men in business suits believe him and young couples cradling their packages believe him and his coffee cup fills and he smiles like he's accomplished something profound.

Ignorant Les is out there too, listening to Bruce.

"I was on a rescue mission in an F-16 when we were shot down. I ejected into the desert."

It dawns on me that as Les's Big Brother, I have a duty to intercede, so I don't know why he looks so surprised when I tug him by the elbow and pull him off to the side.

"He doesn't deserve your money," I say.

Les tries to defend Bruce, but I don't let him get very far.

"I know, it's hard. A guy's spewing at the mouth—making you feel things and you want to help, but really, what is one quarter going to do for him? You know he'll be off to the nearest liquor store when it gets dark out and drink it all away."

"I wasn't giving him money. I was just listening," says Les.

"That's even more dangerous. Give that man a platform and who knows what ideas he'll put into your head. Next time use the back door. It was built to save you from having to make these sorts of decisions."

He nods like he kind of gets it, and I'm proud of myself for taking my Big Brother role seriously, even if I don't like the guy. A dulled quarter is nestled in a small hole in the concrete. Before Bruce can notice it, I quickly pick it up and slip it into my pocket.

At the post office entrance we're waylaid by a small group of protestors with signs accusing our depot of mail theft. Gloria has told us they have a right to be there. I lead Les around to the employee entrance so we don't have to deal with them.

Kimberly arrives at the back door at the same time as us. She stops Les. "Hey! Congratulations! I've never seen it happen so fast!"

"Thanks," Les smiles his oversized smile.

"When do you actually hit the road?" asks Kimberly.

What are they talking about?

We have always made fun of people who think they can climb the ranks so easily.

We stare at the trucks through the window because we know we'll never get there.

"The road?" I ask.

Les nods at Kimberly, who mouths, "Sorry," and walks into the building.

"Gloria thinks it's time I take my exam and become a driver," says Les.

"But you just got a promotion," I say.

"Clerk work isn't for me, Ernest. I like to be out with the people," he says, like he's the fucking pope. "By the way, I'm cooking you dinner tomorrow night, Big Bro."

"I'm busy," I lie.

"I want to celebrate our Bro-hood. I've already planned the menu," he goes on as if he didn't hear me.

Gloria pokes her head out of a doorway, slapping her white comb in the palm of her hand and looks at me.

"Okay, fine. I'll come," I say.

Les gives me a four-fingered wave.

The next morning, I hadn't even made it to my car when Mrs. Newman comes at me with a hoe in hand.

"Do you think I'm an idiot?" she asks.

*Yes, I do*, I want to tell her, but that's no way to start my day. I'm not going to let her get me all riled up. "Rufus has been on lockdown; there's no way he got out again."

"No. My ripe tomatoes have mysteriously disappeared. And I see you have some nice ones resting on your kitchen counter."

Is she seriously accusing me of sneaking into her garden in the middle of the night and stealing her tomatoes?

"You know, they do sell tomatoes at stores, you crazy lady," I say and tip my U.S. Postal Service hat in her direction.

Les's condo is the color of Rufus's tongue. The beak-shaped knocker taps against his door. When it opens, I'm assaulted by the smell of dinner. Les is all smiles, wearing a turquoise apron that says "Real men cook."

"Can I take your man-purse for you?" Les is referring to my satchel. He laughs at himself. "My daughter taught me that word. She's at her grandmother's for the weekend. Wife's gone too."

Les leads me into the living room, where I have a seat on the couch, which is covered in a patchwork quilt. A hodgepodge of baskets line the mantel. The satchel stays at my feet.

"You admiring the baskets? My wife wove them. She can get really tribal." He picks up one and takeout menus fall to the floor. "This one here, it's made out of pine needles. I collected them on my lunch break for two weeks, dried them out, and look what she did with them!"

I pick up one and some needles break off. I quickly place it back in the basket and have a seat on the couch.

"She's in the forest collecting weaving material this weekend. She calls it 'combing out the woods' hair.' Quite beautiful when you think of it. Drink?"

I thought he'd never ask. As Les gets up, there's a loud screech from the dining room.

"What the hell was that?"

"Follow me. I'll get you your drink, and you can meet Twiggy."

He leads me into the dining room and next to the table set for two is a green bird with a bright yellow chest, sitting on its perch in a black cage, scratching itself.

"Here you go. Table red."

After I take the wineglass from him, he clinks his glass against mine and says, "To you, Ernest."

"So, what is that?" I point to the bird.

"Twiggy's a Senegal parrot. We've had her for fifteen years, got her the same year my daughter was born. Raised 'em like twins."

I walk over to the thing and it cocks its head like it's studying me. I'm already imagining the parrot paper cutout I'll have to somehow affix to Les's Big Brother shoulder on the board at work. Les motions me to sit down on the chair next to the bird cage.

"Does it talk?"

"Oh sure. Swears like a sailor sometimes. But she says all sorts of things. 'Hiya, Big Boy' and 'pass the butter'—you know, real cute stuff."

The bird has crazy eyes that grow and shrink as Les talks. It looks possessed.

I think about Rufus and how I can rub his belly, play fetch with him, go for a jog when we were both in better shape. What the hell does Les do with a bird?

We had a special bird stamp series a few years ago: owls, hawks, woodpeckers. I forget what the fourth one was. Part of the proceeds went to saving the animals. They didn't sell very well. Seeing them on letters was the closest I had ever come to a talking bird before tonight.

Les leaves me alone with the bird. From the kitchen, I hear alien sounds—blending, mixing, the oven door creaking open and closed.

After I've helped myself to a second glass of wine, Les makes his grand entrance.

"Chicken in a blueberry reduction sauce." He sticks his finger in the sauce, then puts it in his mouth. "I grew the blueberries myself in the yard."

Who drizzles dessert berries all over perfectly good chicken? He's rendered a fine meal practically inedible. Wait until I tell the others what an idiot he is.

The bird hops off its wooden perch and clasps its claws onto the bars of the cage, right up close to me. Its pupils grow wide.

"What does it eat?"

"I give her vegetables and fruit and special bird tablets."

"So can you give it these leftovers?" I hold up a chicken leg, limp, blue meat dangling off the bone.

"Not really into other human stuff. In fact, even something like chocolate would kill her."

Does Twiggy know I'm eating some distant relative? I can only hope so. I lean toward the bird so that it can watch me chew and swallow.

We talk about work. Les does a good impersonation of Gloria, using a fork to mimic her comb.

Somewhere between the third and fourth glass of wine it occurs to me—*I'm at Les Kunkle's and I'm surviving!*

Then he takes the bird out of the cage, ruining everything.

It's jittery, like a drug addict going through withdrawal.

"Do you want to hold it?" asks Les.

"Absolutely not," I think, but forget to say the words out loud and next thing you know, the bird clutches its claws firmly around my index finger and sidesteps toward my elbow. It leans down and grooms my arm hair with its beak. Les is laughing.

"He's getting to know you."

Then the thing continues moving up my arm quickly.

"Where's it going?"

"She wants a real look at you."

It's on my shoulder now, bobbing its head up and down.

"Wait, I'll be right back . . . gonna get some dessert for us." Les clears the table, then leaves me alone with the bird.

"Hello, Fuckface." I swear it practically whispers in my ear, like it didn't want Les to know it was trash-talking me. I lift my finger up to it. I'm suddenly brave and unafraid, but when I try to pick it up, it nips at my finger. When I shake my shoulder, it only tightens its grasp.

Les places a plate of warm chocolate chip cookies on the table. We both dig in, but he doesn't stay seated for long and soon he's headed toward the kitchen again. I don't want to be left with the bird.

"Just gonna get a treat for Twiggy."

The bird looks at me. "I love you," it says creepily. Bipolar bird. Could Twiggy be possessed by my ex-wife? I hold out a chocolate chip to the bird. He hops over to it and starts to investigate, then pecks at it and swallows.

Les comes back with a handful of sunflower seeds and the bird shimmies down my arms and across the table, and then over to its owner, who has a goddamn sunflower seed in his mouth that the bird grabs and opens, sending the shell falling to the table.

"Watch this, you'll love it." Les opens his mouth and the bird runs beak first, head in mouth, and starts picking at the food between Les's teeth. It's the vilest thing I've ever seen in my life.

"I think I need to use the restroom."

"The downstairs toilet was giving me problems this morning. Try the one upstairs, through our bedroom."

Grabbing my satchel, I follow Les's suggestion. The leather strap feels cool on my fingers. I've had too much to drink.

The bathroom has his and hers sinks. His toothbrushes stick out of one of his wife's woven baskets. It reeks of Les's aftershave in here. Makes me nauseous.

After relieving myself, I have a seat on the toilet.

The letters call to me. Better than a passport.

As though I'm picking numbered balls for the lottery, I reach in to see the lucky winner: no stickers, plain brown envelope. Must have grabbed this one by accident. The stamp features President Roosevelt sitting with pride in his wheelchair. I wonder if the recipient is in a wheelchair? Is the sender mocking her? Clever.

Tearing open the envelope, the crisp paper crackles as I unfold it.

*"Dear Grandma. I am so so sorry. Please forgive me. I love you, Greg."*

I think about his grandma—a woman I've never met, lying in a bed underneath a cross on the wall, breathing shallow breaths, waiting for an apology.

Checking the return address, I see it's from Greg Garrison. I know him. This is the letter Gloria was talking about. This familiarity with the writer kills the whole endeavor.

It would be so easy to leave all the letters here and then call in an anonymous tip. Let Les take the fall.

Then we can get back to work.

"You okay up there?" Les calls.

Just peachy.


Les is eating another cookie and stroking Twiggy, who is lying belly up on his lap. He pinches the side of her neck with his thumb and forefinger and gently rubs the feathers back and forth. The bird looks like it's in a trance.

It's after nine.

"I gotta get back to my dog." The doctor told me it's real important to be consistent with the meds.

"Already? I thought we could play some cards?"

I shrug.

Les's eyes stay fixed on the bird.

"Well, thanks for dinner. I'll see you at work. Or, I guess not since you're switching departments. Hey, is there any leftover chicken? For my dog."

Les nods and disappears into the kitchen, then emerges with some pieces in a plastic bag. It will be fine after a good rinse at home to remove the residual blueberry.

"I take my exam next Saturday, so keep your fingers crossed." His nub doesn't make it over his index finger. What's the point of performing an act of superstition if you can't even do it right? Twiggy ambles up his fingers and then hangs upside down—but then falls face first on the table.

"That's not like her. She usually has great balance." Les puts her back in her cage and she huddles in the corner.

When we get to the door, I turn to Les, who has his back to the kitchen. The bird is dry heaving, but Les doesn't notice because he's busy telling me what a great time he had.

The night has grown cool. The wind blows leaves and pine needles across his brick stairs. My shoulder feels light without the weight of my satchel.

"Thanks, Big Bro," Les reaches out his hand to shake mine. I take hold and while grasping, sneak my index finger in to the warm area where our palms meet, desperately feeling for the missing nub of his finger. I find the tip that sinks below his other digits. It wiggles like a lizard that's just lost its tail.

# The Dolphinarium

---

## 1967

Reva was surprised to discover that James was odorless. She assumed he'd smell like fish. She met all five dolphins at the same time, but it was James who raised his beak out of the water and really stared at her. No one had looked into her eyes with such earnestness for a long time.

"He's flirting with you," said Kip, a burning doobie hanging out the left side of his mouth that flapped up and down as he spoke. "He thinks you're groovy."

Reva was groovy. Her hair cascaded down her back like a waterfall. Her floral muumuu concealed a tiny figure beneath. The freckles on Reva's ruddy cheeks gave her the whimsical air of a ten-year-old, even though she was nineteen.

She had met Kip waitressing at the Crab Shack a few days earlier. He had asked what was good.

"Fish tacos," she replied.

"I hate fish," he said and ordered a bloody mary instead.

After Kip had chewed the celery to a green pulp, he told her about the Aquatic Center.

"We're a group of researchers. We received a grant to work with dolphins."

"I'd love to check it out," said Reva, her breath quickening.

Kip got up and placed his finger on Reva's exposed sternum.

"See you soon," he said, handing her his card before leaving her in front of the plywood mural of an underwater scene that was the Crab Shack's backdrop.

Her afternoon with the dolphins had been magical. Kip showed off every trick in the book. The bottlenosed-dolphins jumped through hoops. They spat water at her face on cue (it was endearing.) James waved his pectoral fin. Reva waved back.

But she could tell by the way the sun sank closer to the ocean that her waitressing shift would start soon. "I have to go," she told Kip, who tossed a mackerel into Jacob's mouth. The dolphin snagged it at the back of his jaws and swam off.

A few days later, when Reva visited the Aquatic Center a second time, Kip held out a bucket of fish.

"Want to feed them?"

Reva had been feeding people all day. But this was different. These pescatarians ate with fervor and appreciation. They didn't criticize her service or demand to speak with the manager.

"You should quit your waitressing job and work here. We could use more bodies," said Kip.

"What's he doing?" Reva asked when she noticed James rubbing his body against the side of the tank.

"He's a teenager. He's horny, like me."

She stayed the afternoon and Kip opened a bottle of cheap chablis. They drank it by the tank, smoked a joint, and made out as the odor of the fish from the bucket crept into Reva's nostrils and over her hair and wet Birkenstocks.

The dolphins remained odorless.

Reva approached the Aquatic Center for the third time while carrying two suitcases and an orange lava lamp.

"We're not open to the public," Kip told her while his arm was around an even younger version of Reva.

"I quit my job," she said, walking closer so Kip would recognize her.

"That was fast," said Kip, moving his hand to massage the new girl's neck.

The new girl giggled. "Put her in the Dolphinarium."

Reva went with the flow. "What's a Dolphinarium?"

"You ever dreamed of being a dolphin when you were a kid?" asked Kip.

Reva thought about it. She dreamed about a lot of things when she was little. She thought about how unfair it was that her mother had expected her to be a dutiful housewife while her brother had a job waiting for him, working alongside her father on Wall Street, when he finished college. Reva had dreamed about moving to a co-op and raising chickens. She had dreamed of escaping the noise and pollution and rules of New York City and she made that dream come true. But never once had she dreamed about being a dolphin.

"No," said Reva.

"Well, your dreams are about to come true," said Kip dismissively, leading her to a one-storey concrete building, a five-minute walk from the dolphin tank.

Inside a second set of doors, water rushed up to her thighs. Reva hoisted her now-damp dress above the waterline.

"You're gonna have to lose the muumuu," said Kip. "You've got four feet of water throughout. There's a deeper pool James can swim to off the kitchen if he wants more depth, but he'll mostly want to be wherever you are. Like a dog."

The interior looked just like a studio apartment. The desk was suspended from the ceiling with bungee cables. A mattress sat well above the waterline on a plastic platform. There was a kitchenette with a teakettle and a mini-fridge. But to navigate between these various areas, she would definitely have to get wet.

"I don't understand. What am I doing here?"

"You're going to live here with James. You're going to teach him things," said Kip.

"Like what?"

"Like . . ." Kip thought for a moment as though he didn't even know what the goal of this scientific experiment was. "Like how to count. Let's start with that," he said, as though mammalian mathematics was no gigantic feat. She was familiar with numbers. Her brother used to be a numbers guy.

## 1962

Reva's brother was home from college. His face shone like a newly polished bowling ball. All of her dad's friends shook his hand as they arrived at the cocktail party. They patted him on the back and made crude jokes about how he must spend his free time on weekends, then proceeded to tell him stories of what certain girls had done to them in the backs of cars, under bleachers, and in whorehouses.

Reva remained invisible to these men. She wore her hair up in a bun, a leftover habit from her early childhood days as a ballet student, when her only goal had been to move through space. She'd wrapped her toes so tightly to fit into her pointe shoes that she lost all semblance of being a ten-toed creature. She was just a foot of flesh. A gastropod—like a snail.

"Come on," said John, grabbing Reva and pulling her outside when no one was looking. They ran to the fire exit and up the stairs from the penthouse to the rooftop. Straight ahead was Central Park, dimly lit under the New York skyline.

"It's all ours out there," John told her. "Ours for the taking."

"You mean it's yours, John."

"What are you talking about, kid?" He gave her shoulder a slight shove.

"Dad's not offering me a job. He's not letting me work!"

"You're lucky!" said John.

Reva just wanted John to see things the way she did.

"You'll be fine," John continued. "And besides, you'll always have me."

Reva felt a comfort with her brother that she never felt with other boys.

"Here," he said, "try this." He took out what looked like a fat cigarette from his pants pocket and lit it. He began puffing, causing the end to burn quickly.

"What is that?" she asked. She had stolen her mother's cigarettes before. But they were thin. And menthol. This version was overstuffed and smelled like sage.

"Just try some." He passed the funny-smelling cigarette to her and she imitated his movements, inhaling deeply. But instead of doing it gracefully as her brother had, her lungs rejected the smoke and she began to cough uncontrollably.

He laughed.

"What is this, John?"

"It's a revolution."

She tried again and this time, the smoke went down more smoothly. Soon, she was giggling and staring at the city lights, which looked like stars.

"The galaxy is big," she told her brother.

"Which means that we're really, really small," he said.

She wanted to stay on that rooftop and be minuscule with him forever.

## 1967

There were no cranes or pulleys to move James from his tank to his new digs with Reva. All twenty team members at the Aquatic Center worked together to lift the adolescent dolphin out of the water and into a harness. His tail, sticking out the back end, slipped out of their hands only once, throwing them all off-balance before they proceeded down some stairs and across the grounds to the Dolphinarium.

"Home sweet home?" Reva asked herself. She was wearing a knee-length sleeveless jumper. James explored his new environment. The others wanted to linger inside.

"This is just for Reva," said Kip, ushering everyone out.

Reva sat down at her desk and opened the blank journal that had been left on top. "First Impressions:" she wrote. "I'm living with a sea animal." She thought about her junior roommate at boarding school—a square named Tiffany, who woke up at six in the morning to get her hair into the perfect beehive. Reva had wanted to release a swarm of bees into that hair. She wanted to shred Tiffany's mod skirt suits and burn her geometric drapes. But instead, Reva dropped out of prep school and ran away to the dot her finger found on a map, right in the middle of the country, mathematically the farthest space from any oceans.

James swam under her desk. Reva lifted her feet out of the water, afraid he'd mistake her toes for trout. He paused under her like a begging dog, so she reached into the water to pet him. He felt so rubbery, like a peeled hard-boiled egg. James opened his mouth as if to smile. Was he smiling?

Their first night together was awkward. Reva slept in shorts and a tank top and fell asleep to the sound of water lapping against the acrylic walls as James circled his way around the room repeatedly.

In the middle of the night he spat water at her.

"Huh?" She had forgotten where she was. "No, not now, James," she said, opening one eye. "I need to sleep."

James whistled. She shooed him away. He whistled again, this time with urgency. She couldn't say no. He wanted her. She rolled off her bed straight into the water and laughed at the absurdity of it all before playing a version of tag with James that lasted until the sun crept up.

Reva had been living in the Dolphinarium for three weeks. She slept in bathing suits. It was easier to be on-call this way. Her hair was bunched in a permanent bun. No progress had been made in the math department, but Reva and James had slipped into a daily routine. Each morning she'd roll right into the water at James's urgings and they'd alternate between moments of play and rest for most of the day. By nightfall, her skin would be prune-like, her sebum lost to the water.

Her journal was full of observations and inquiries. All science started with a question and she was eager to add to them: Did James have a sibling? Do dolphins mourn?

This morning she made herself a cup of Earl Grey, which was one of the only habits she still cherished from childhood, the ritual of tea. The tea bag slipped off the table and into the water. Before she could grab it, James discovered it and gently placed it in his beak. He clicked at it, using his sonar to size up the foreign object.

James threw the tea bag against the wall and watched in wide-eyed delight as it slid down the wall and plopped back into the water. He then catapulted the bag up higher on the wall and clicked once in anticipation of its fall.

Was this gurgled version of a monosyllabic word his sound for "one"? Was he counting? Or could it have been his version of the word "tea"? Maybe he was counting the bag: one. Whatever meaning was behind the utterance, Reva was floored. "Say it again!" she encouraged. James obliged with a singular chortle.

"Yes!" she said and swam as fast as she could to the bucket of fish in the refrigerator.

When he had gulped down his fish, he went back to the tea bag, this time more aggressively. He threw it on the wall and watched it fall. He threw it across the room and retrieved it. He dexterously grabbed the bag and shook it aggressively between his teeth. Much to his surprise, the bag tore, sending bits of tea leaves floating through the water. James spent the rest of the day sonaring each and every single one of them.

At night, John came to Reva in a dream. He was wearing a U.S. Army uniform. His head was shaved and he was sweating. He smiled at his sister before vanishing. It was James who had awakened her—a spouting water fountain.

"Do you have an electric razor?" she asked Kip when she was granted an afternoon off to buy some toothpaste and feel the sunlight.

"Sure. I'll go get it. In the meantime, do you want some?" He took an envelope from his jeans pocket and produced what looked like a sheet of stamps with a repeating image of a dolphin over a rainbow. He tore two squares off and handed them to her.

"What is that?"

"Give it to James. It's acid. I've been giving it to the ladies in the upper tank. They go nuts for this shit. We're all doing it together tonight. Dolphins and humans. You should join us."

Reva placed the acid in her pocket, but as soon as she was out of sight, she let it fall to the ground.

That night, she sat on her dry bed and ran the razor through her long hair. She watched as it dropped to the blanket. Hair was so quiet.

"Now we're twins."

James nodded.

She covered her head in a Crab Shack sweatshirt and snuck outside to one of the outdoor tanks. It sounded like a party. Kip was in the center of the tank, passing a joint to other researchers. The dolphins circled them, swimming sluggishly. The new girl exhaled smoke into a dolphin's exposed blowhole. Reva wanted to grab James and run away, but the logistics stymied her and instead, she returned to the Dolphinarium, seeking refuge in sleep.

As she slumbered, Reva's hand dipped into the water. The sudden wetness on her hand woke her. When she opened her eyes, James was at her side, exploring her hand, which remained submerged. He sonared in the space between her fingers as if to say, "What are those things you have?" She put her other hand in and he did the same. Five sonars. She dunked her feet in and ten sonars later he was looking at her and clicking. She couldn't explain hands to a dolphin. She couldn't explain anything to him. The longer she stayed in the Dolphinarium, the less she knew about what it meant to be a human.

# 1963

Reva and her family had gone to their summer home in the Hamptons right before John was to report to the enlisting officer. The sky looked as though it was on fire. Her belly was full of lobster and the Châteauneuf-du-Pape her brother passed her, which she chugged when her parents had left the room. Later, on the beach, the siblings shared a joint.

Surf advisory warnings were posted up and down the beach. Riptides. Violent waves.

Reva buried her legs under a pile of sand.

"You look like a mermaid," John said.

"It's freezing, I'm going back in. You coming?" Reva stood up.

"I'm going to wait until the sun goes down. It's my last sunset on this coast for a while."

"Suit yourself," Reva said, heading home. Halfway back to the house, the pot hit her hard. The beach grass tickled her legs as she ran past and she had an urgent need to know how the grass grew in the sand. There wasn't soil. Who watered it? Had someone planted it or was it au natural? She needed answers. Her brother would know. She ran full speed back to the beach, but her brother was gone.

A pod of dolphins swam past. A straggler who had fallen behind was trying to catch up. They swam with such speed and determination. They seemed to know exactly where they were going. She wished she had their confidence in direction. She followed them north, until her gaze caught a figure atop the rocks that jutted out above the ocean. When they were kids they used to climb up to that same spot and look for hermit crabs and fish that had become trapped in small tide pools in the crags of the rocks.

It was John, his lean body silhouetted against the setting sun. Then he dove into the water.

His body would be recovered two days later, washed ashore. Bloated and puckered. His blue eyes, brown. His pale skin, blue.

# 1967

Before she had the opportunity to share James's counting skills with the world, before she had a chance to say good-bye to her underwater friend, word leaked out about the unorthodox methods being applied to the animals at the Aquatic Center. Men had come in vans to gather the dolphins and relocate them to various marine parks throughout the country.

James would be moved to Montana.

Their strides in communication would remain a secret between the two of them.

She didn't even get a chance to say good-bye.

Reva headed back to the Crab Shack to beg for her job, pausing at the plywood mural of tropical fish. Blooming anemone and a lone dolphin were missing paint in places. The entire piece reminded her of a gift her brother had once given her for her birthday—an ocean-themed paint-by-numbers project she never completed. Blue chips of paint lay scattered like confetti at her feet.

# Unruly

———

The train's only job is to stay on track. Not deviate. Complete its revolution.

It takes seven minutes and thirty-nine seconds for the train to go around the tracks. The front car, a miniature version of a steam engine, is the color of bile and tows eight passenger cars, each equipped with five small benches. Each bench seats two people or, as is the case sometimes, one really fat one. Caroline has been a conductor at the Salty Dog Train ride, the most popular attraction in Paradise Park, all summer. She needed a job, an excuse to get out of her home, which she affectionately calls "The Bog."

In the ticket booth, Caroline reaches above Rusty's bald spot, into the cabinet, for a red-and-white striped conductor's hat. None of the hats fit her wide head properly, so she comes armed with her own metal clips to put the hat into lockdown.

Across the tracks, past the scaled-down soccer field, Tom operates the merry-go-round. Today is his first day back from work after his accident.

Rusty put his hands on Caroline's shoulders two weeks ago. "I have some bad news, kid. It's Tom. Flipped his car four times. We've gotta pray our hardest for him."

According to Rusty, Tom still has window glass embedded in his arms. Pieces surface, like crops in a garden, ready to be picked.

The stiff horses go around in circles and Caroline looks on as Tom pinches and picks at his skin, trying to retrieve hidden shards.

At home Caroline takes off her overalls in her bedroom and her pubic hair spills over her thighs, where it hangs like tassels on a loincloth. Her breath quickens, her throat feels dry. She hesitantly reaches down to touch the hair to make sure it's real.

This morning she was just a regular girl with regular girl body hair.

She pulls on a pair of sweatpants and rushes into the kitchen, drawing the shades. Luckily her mom isn't home. With the scissors from the knife block, Caroline cuts off the hair. It rests in her palm like wilted flower stems. She washes it down the sink and turns on the disposal. The blades turn, chopping the hair into a fine clump of mush, floating through the pipes out to sea.

A large terrarium takes up most of the kitchen table.

"Great," thinks Caroline. "They've infiltrated."

Her mom is a biologist at a local university, specializing in toad and frog reproduction, and used to make a big deal about "not taking work home," but later it was as though work became her addiction and frogs her version of crack. Now there's a small lab set up in her home office and aquariums and terrariums rest on most available surfaces. This new one makes habitat number twelve.

The note on the table reads:

*Won't be home in time for supper. There's canned soup or meatloaf you can microwave.*

*Hugs and ribbits,*
*Mom*

Caroline peers through the glass at the toads. Three fat ones sit, looking like craggy stones, their bellies pulsing. One turns a little to the left. Lucky to be hairless.

"Next stop, New York City!" Caroline's passengers cheer after she makes the announcement into the intercom. She picks a different destination for every ride, studies her bedroom carpet, shaped like a map of the United States. New York, half covered by her laundry hamper, is always a crowd pleaser.

"How can we get to New York if we're just going in a circle?" Christopher, a Salty Dog regular, asks his mother, who holds him so tightly it looks like she may smother him.

Caroline checks to see whether everyone is seated before turning the switch that starts the engine. She presses a yellow button. Passengers' voices echo the sound of the whistle and they begin to chug along past the pony rides. The track weaves and climbs, lurching toward Tom's post at the merry-go-round. The proximity excites her. He's helping a girl put her feet in fake stirrups. The train keeps moving.

The pubic hair seemed under control this morning. Maybe it was all a hallucination. Maybe someone slipped something in her soda at work.

Caroline scratches at her inner thigh. Last summer she had poison oak. It covered her legs in faded pink splotches, like the cartography of some unknown world. Her mother dipped her in calamine lotion and milk baths, which always stung before they soothed.

"Once we took a trip to the ocean. Your dad got bit by a jellyfish. I had to pee on him to take the burn out. "

After the ride, Caroline goes to the bathroom and takes off her overalls. She pulls down her underwear and the hair spills out to her knees, hanging like the limp, synthetic hair on a doll. She has to hold it up with two hands while she urinates—has to make sure it doesn't accidentally get flushed down the toilet, pulling her skin off with it. Toilet scalping. She is finding new hazards every day.

"All aboard!" Rusty yells outside to the growing line, which snakes around all the way to the Disaster Simulator. It's Caroline's cue to get back to her post. She quickly gathers the hair and stuffs it back into her underwear. It bulges unevenly. It slips out the sides.

"Stay!" Caroline pleads as though the hair was a naughty puppy. She puts her overalls back on, thankful they are roomy enough to hide her secret.

At home her mother looks small, sleeping alone in the king-sized bed. Caroline can't remember what the bed looked like when her father shared it. He left when she was only four.

"The man's a genetic mystery," her mom told her whenever Caroline used to ask about him.

The toads that her mom now calls The Three Tenors croak. In a neighboring aquarium, fresh tadpoles swim around like misplaced musical notes, their tails flagellating. She wonders how something can go from tadpole to frog with no effort.

Caroline's mom doesn't know that her one and only daughter doesn't plan on going back to college. Her grades were mediocre and her motivation nonexistent. Her mom expects her to be a scientist or a doctor.

"You may never get to the truth, but you should always investigate," said her mother while peering at frog cell division under her high-resolution microscope.

The pipes whine as the water pours into the bathtub. Since there's no bubble bath, she pretends the green dish soap from the kitchen is the real stuff and gives it a good squeeze as she fills the tub. The bubbles make a thick foam, like the kind she once saw spewing from the mouth of a rabid squirrel in the park at the beginning of summer. The ranger was called and he shot it once in the head.

"Have to keep the people safe," he explained.

Caroline examines her bare chest in the mirror.

"Pear or apple shaped?" she once read in a magazine. Caroline thinks that she looks more like a strawberry, plump at the shoulders with large legs that narrow into small, unsteady ankles. She takes off the rest of her clothing and the pubic hair unfurls, thicker than before, past her thighs. Caroline tries to hold back tears.

Wrapped in a towel in case her mother wakes up, she goes to the kitchen and grabs a knife; the scissors have proven useless. The knife clinks against the aquarium and the tadpoles scatter and then regroup. In the bathroom, Caroline begins cutting off chunks of the hair, straddling the toilet, hoping the hair will fall down on target, to be flushed away, no evidence left behind.

The hair first showed up when she was in the seventh grade, dark, emerging, one strand at a time. Then more hair grew, covering her pale pubic area with scraggly locks. Her period came a week later.

After that, pus-filled pimples started appearing on her face and back. She would pick at them for hours, pretending she was a surgeon—would even put their contents on a glass slide under her mother's microscope in secret, amazed to see a part of her up close, viscous and creamy.

Caroline imagined her pimples as tiny fish eyes covering her body. She'd pretend she could see behind her. Watch her back.

Now, dark hairs scatter over the tile of the bathroom floor. Caroline wets a wad of toilet paper and tries to pick them up. By the time she makes it to the tub, the water is no longer warm, which wouldn't matter a lick if she were amphibious.

"Today, we'll be visiting the Everglades."

"What's that?" asks Christopher, who has chosen the seat directly behind Caroline.

"It's in Florida," explains his mom.

"It's like a swamp," says Caroline.

"Trains can't ride through swamps." Christopher crosses his arms in disappointment.

Caroline starts the engine. "This one can."

"Are there frogs?"

It always came back to frogs.

"Carrie, can you go get Tom's timecard?" Rusty asks when she returns from her loop. She used to hate it when he called her that, but now she sees it as a term of endearment.

"Want some popcorn?" Tom hands her his timecard from the back of his red pants pocket. It's warm, almost moist, like it could be torn without making a ripping sound.

She shakes her head. They stand there in silence, watching the horses go around and around, up and down. Her eyes stay focused on the one with a purple saddle and a golden flowing mane. Tom pulls up the sleeve of his red shirt and fingers his left arm, back and forth, like he's strumming a ukulele. His flesh is covered in cuts and dried blood. She's about to ask him what it felt like to flip his car and spin out of control, but then the music stops and the horses slow.

"That's my cue." Tom walks back to his station, but his arms pump as though he is running.

The hair itches as Caroline rides the bus home. She covers her lap with her jacket, sneaks her hands under the wool fabric and starts scratching vigorously. She feels the hair through her overalls, gathering in uneven clumps.

The man across the aisle shakes his head and gets off at the next exit.

At home she lies on her back on her bedroom carpet, unclips her overalls and slides them off. The hair covers Kentucky and spills down to Tennessee. She grabs a section of her foreign mane and moves a larger kitchen knife, a serrated one this time, back and forth in a sawing motion, switching directions only when a frog croaks. It's a game of restraint. The hair breaks away. If she were creative, she could make something with the hair—a lanyard, a bookmark. Instead, she carefully pulls a clump of strands away from the bunch and hides the rest in the trash can. She wishes she could talk to her mom about these things, but she never can seem to find the right time.

She listens for clues that her mom has returned—coffee percolating in the kitchen, aquarium lids sliding on and off. Nothing. She holds the saved strands in front of her, like one might carry a mouse by the tail, down the hall to her mother's office, wearing only a t-shirt and underwear. Without the excess hair she feels lighter. She pulls a laboratory stool from under the desk, and flips the red switch that starts the motor of the high-power compound microscope. Caroline takes a fresh slide from a small cardboard box. She isolates three strands of hair and places them on the slide.

The frogs croak. It's like Chinese water torture.

She puts a flexible plastic film over the slide, sandwiching the hairs. Magnified, the hairs look like prehistoric worms found deep in the ground. Each hair is covered with scales, like armor. The frogs sing in a drunken chorus.

"Anyone home? Great news! I harvested a blastocyte today!"

Caroline quickly turns off the microscope and hides the slide in her hand. Panicking, she gathers the rest of the hair. As she hops off the stool, she glances down and sees the newly grown hair already overflowing out of the top and leg holes of her underwear, cascading down her legs, tickling her shins.

"Aloha! We're going to Hawaii today!" Caroline presses the whistle button twice, excited by her selected destination.

When she woke up this morning, the growth seemed to have stalled, the follicles perhaps depleted from yesterday's spurt.

"That's an island." Christopher reminds her. "You can't get there by train."

The conductor isn't supposed to talk back. "If they sass you, they sass you," Rusty always tells her when she complains.

They chug past a field of wild flowers, then over a small bridge and through a tunnel where kids' screams reverberate in cochleae.

After the ride she gives the wheels and cogs a once-over to see if there are any *visible signs of fatigue*. Halfway down the cars she sees something shiny on the wheel and reaches down to fish it out. Just a tangled balloon ribbon. She carefully unravels the ribbon and pulls it loose. Her hands are covered in sticky black oil.

"You look like a car mechanic," Christopher says, waiting in line to ride the train again. Luckily her shift is over.

"Hey, Caroline, I want you to meet a new member of our team." To Rusty's left is a girl who resembles a Popsicle stick, tall and rangy.

"This is Candy. Funny thing is . . . she's going to be selling cotton candy. I didn't even think of that until now."

Candy's smile is wide. She pops her blue gum.

"She's just starting out. I thought you could be a mentor to her. Teach her the ropes. Show her where the locker room is. I'll go and get the candy maker . . . for Candy." Rusty shakes his head, laughing to himself.

She walks Candy to the dressing rooms and shows her the uniform. Treat Girls wear red velvet hot pants and a white tank top.

"I was pushing a cart over by the pier, but I guess sales were low so they canned me. You like it here?"

Candy sits on a bench, tugging at her knee high. The overalls, coupled with the hair, are making Caroline overheat. She wants to change out of her uniform, but doesn't want to run the risk of Candy seeing the hair when she takes it off. She turns away from the new girl and drops the overalls to the floor, the metal clasps clinking. Hair plunges down to Caroline's ankles.

"I know someone who can fix that."

Caroline feels her jaw tighten.

"You're not the only one, you know. We have it in my family too. My great-aunt, my sister. Go to the pier, to the nail shop. Ask for Fang-Fang." Candy snaps the rim of her socks, once on each side, before leaving Caroline alone.

When her mother is asleep, Caroline brings a flashlight with her to bed and turns it on under the covers, like she's camping. She takes off her pajama bottoms and wriggles out of her underwear. In bed the hair clings to her legs like ivy wrapped around an aging building. She thinks of it as an *other*—like that plant in that musical that takes over and terrorizes the town. But her own hair doesn't sing, just lies there like moss on a rock, existing. In biology class she learned that a single strand contains the entire genetic makeup for an organism. She reaches down to touch it, first singling out strands, following them from where they emerge from the skin to where they end. There are no straight lines, each hair has its own crooked path, individual, like fingerprints. She grabs hold of the entire mass and moves her fingers over it—a horse's tail.

Caroline finds a knot and reaches for the hairbrush on her bedside table. She moves the brush in deliberate strokes through the hair. She comes across a lump and sits up quickly and reaches down with one hand. With the other, she grabs the flashlight and focuses. It's a brilliant blue-and-black tree frog mid-metamorphosis, tail still present, halfway between two lives. Her mother doesn't work with these frogs; they're found only in the Amazon. There's no place to return it. She jumps out of bed and turns the light on to check and see if there are others, but it appears to be the only one. She holds it around its throbbing abdomen, opens her bedroom window, and flattens her palm. The frog leaps to a nearby branch.

After work the next day, Caroline makes her way to the pier, not sure how she will explain her problem to whomever helps her. She walks quickly past a barbershop with the candy-cane pole rotating out front. A bell tied to the door tings as she enters the nail shop. Inside, ethyl acetate wafts over the room. Women tend to women, painting nails and toes loud colors, buffing calluses off feet, and cutting cuticles.

"You want Fang-Fang?" A beautician shouts. Caroline wonders what gave her away. She nods. The woman points to the back of the salon where three chairs sit outside a door marked "Private." A woman holds her daughter's hand. She has tears in her eyes. Her mother passes the girl a tissue. Caroline takes a seat next to them. The door opens and Fang-Fang emerges. She looks at Caroline, then the girl.

"You first," she says to Caroline. "Look like a quick one." Before the girl's mother can protest, Fang-Fang leads her into a room that smells of incense.

Fang-Fang wastes no time. "You take off your pants and put these on." She hands Caroline a sheet to cover herself up with, like she's at the gynecologist, and then leaves the room. Caroline does as she's told, but the hair pushes its way out of the paper, ripping it like a present opening itself from the inside.

After a staccato knock the woman reenters, wearing surgical gloves. She takes one look at Caroline, draws in a deep breath, and releases it slowly, mindfully.

"I'll cut it off, then wax it. Big job. More money."

Caroline nods.

Fang-Fang pulls out small sheers and snips quickly with the precision of a gardener working on a topiary. Caroline doesn't want to watch. Just wants the whole procedure over with. After the hair is shorn, out comes the hot wax. Caroline likes the way it burns as it's applied, stinging in one place first, then radiating out to the surrounding skin. But the ripping, which sounds like Velcro, feels like a dive into a pile of stinging nettles.

She looks at the lettering on Fang-Fang's name tag and thinks of a vampire sucking her blood.

Fang-Fang sweeps the pile of hair from the floor and puts it in a plastic bag.

"We'll donate this. For kids with no hair." She lowers her voice to a whisper. "Won't tell where it came from." Her smile erupts into a laugh.

Caroline imagines some sad cancer patient, small and suffering, being given a wig of her scraggly pubic hair. They're lucky to have it. Let the hair be someone else's problem.

Fang-Fang gives Caroline a handheld mirror and leaves the room. She lowers the mirror and angles it upward so she can see her new image. The hair is all gone. She strokes the bumpy, bare surface, relishing the skin-to-skin contact.

As she leaves the room, the girl on the chair looks at her, asking with her eyes if the treatment was bearable. Caroline is about to speak, but doesn't know what to say. Instead she emits a wheezing groan that causes the girl to fold into her mother's arms.

A week later, it's timecard day again. When Caroline reaches Tom, he's pouring kernels into the metal popper.

"Stand back. This thing gets hot."

Caroline's not scared. But then he rolls up his shirtsleeve and any lines rehearsed in her head vanish. His fingers move up then down his arm as the corn begins to pop, sporadically at first and then in synch with the kernels cooking. He stops at a spot halfway between his elbow and wrist. He pinches the skin. Caroline watches. When the glass emerges, she feels a rush and a dryness in her throat. He momentarily lets it sit on his skin before flicking the piece onto the ground. She wonders how something so fascinating to her can be so casual to him.

"You want this or what?"

How long has he been standing there with the timecard? Caroline takes the paper from him as a couple asks for a large order of popcorn to share. While he's distracted, she scans the ground for the piece of glass, carefully picks it up, and puts it in the front pocket of her overalls.

At home, Caroline rushes to her mother's microscope and hits the switch. The motor runs and it heats quickly. Pulling a slide under the light, she carefully places the glass from Tom's arm on the microscope's surface.

She lowers her head to the metal eyepiece and adjusts the coarse and fine focus knobs until the image changes from blurry to clear. The glass is more opaque than she thought it would be. It looks like a geological site, with its own ridges and cavities. There are no droplets of Tom's blood as she had hoped. But she is surprised by a small fissure in the upper right-hand corner that extends halfway down the glass and wonders if the crack occurred while inside his arm or at the time of the accident.

The glass is a recorded history.

She wants to tell Tom about what she's discovered about his glass— tell him how beautiful she thinks it is. She wants to spend a night prying at his arm and saving the pieces.

A catastrophe that almost was.

It's sweltering outside. A true summer day. The body hair is back, now down to the floor. The money she spent on Fang-Fang yesterday was a waste. Stepping across her room, Caroline feels something soft and squishy under her toes. She lifts her left foot. Brown frog droppings. There's a trail of poop that moves up the east coast of her carpet to the bathroom. In the bathroom, there's a note on the sink.

*Off to my conference. Be back in three days. Watch over my babies for me. Sorry about your tub. Mine's full.*

*Love,*
*Mom*

Caroline slides open the shower door. Inside, an orgy of frogs sits restlessly. As she slams the door shut, a frog attempts to make its great escape and gets crushed at the belly in the door. The legs stick out. She's heard they're considered a delicacy in some parts.

Back in her room, she rushes to get dressed. She now has a practiced routine for stuffing the hair into her overalls. She grabs it at the base and begins twisting it into a rope. Once she reaches the end, she begins to twist the hair into a tight bun. Once the bun is in place, she puts on the heavy overalls.

"Today, we are going to keep it close to home and go to . . . Paradise Park," she announces to her first batch of riders on this crowded Saturday morning.

"That's not fair," yells Christopher sitting in the car directly behind Caroline. His mother nervously spins her wedding ring.

Caroline whirls around to look at him. She's had enough of his whining. "And it's gonna be a fast one."

The train leaves the safety of the station and begins its circular path through the park.

On the first revolution, Caroline sees Tom with his arm around Candy. The two are laughing, their bodies pressed up against one another. Caroline needs more details. She takes the train around a second time.

"Round two!" Caroline cranks the lever into high gear.

"I want to get off!" Christopher says, then starts to cry.

Caroline cranks up the speed as high as the lever will go. The train creaks and moans in ways she's never heard.

"Mom, what is that?" Christopher asks.

She feels it before she sees it. There's a gap in Caroline's overalls and the hair is out, loose, making its way into the rest of the train. It engulfs Christopher and then his mother, their voices muffled by the aggressive strands. It moves toward the back of the train without discrimination. The train is now a hairy express.

Families around her are running away, screaming, holding their children, dropping their cotton candy.

As she chugs past the far side of the soccer field, the red lump that is Tom gets larger and larger, as does Candy, standing next to him, head tilted, smile ignited. She snaps her knee-highs and then puts both hands on Tom's arm.

The hair has wound itself around the wheels and the train seizes and stops. They look up at all the noise. Candy starts to run, but the hair catches and then engulfs her.

Tom stays still. It's what you're supposed to do if a shark approaches you in the water. The hair rises above him next to a sign that reads "Ducks Crossing." And then, he's gone.

Caroline steps out of the train and walks toward the pavement in front of the carousel while the hair continues to spread out over the entire acreage of the park, wrapping itself around trees, billowing over buildings, swing sets, a park ranger.

Forest animals, sensing the danger, make a dash for higher ground. Some make it.

Caroline, seemingly floating on the unforgiving tresses through the carnage like Botticelli's Venus, pushes through the hair covering the ground until she finds the spot next to the sign where Tom had stood.

Reaching down, like a kid hunting sand crabs at the beach, she fumbles for broken glass, picking up the shards one at a time and placing them in her overall's double chest pocket. There's no telling what she might discover when it's examined at two hundred times original size.

# Reading Questions

———

1. While the eleven stories in *Unruly Creatures* are not overtly connected to one another, can you identify some of the overarching themes in this collection?

2. Some of these stories present as reinterpretations of various fairy tales. Identify which stories may be rooted in fairy tales. How are Caloyeras's stories different from and similar to the original tales?

3. Many of the stories incorporate the use of surrogates: in "A Real Live Baby" a doll is a substitute for a baby; in "Plush," a young adult must dress in costume in order to receive affection from his father. What other stories have instances of surrogacy and what function do you think this serves?

4. Some of these stories deal with dissatisfaction toward and betrayal by characters' own bodies (such as "Unruly," "Roadkill," and "Bloodletting"). Discuss how the protagonists' bodies have let them down in each of these stories and whether or not nature or nurture is at play in each circumstance.

5. A few of these stories ("Unruly," "A Real Live Baby," and "Stuffed") may be considered coming-of-age stories. How do they fit in this genre and what can they tell us about bourgeoning adulthood?

6. Identity is another theme throughout this collection. Stories like "Roadkill," "Big Brother," and "Plush" explore this theme in different ways. Discuss the ways in which identity is addressed in these stories.

7. How is the environment portrayed in the various landscapes of these stories?

8. Many stories deal with relationships that people have with the animal world. "The Sound of an Infinite Gesture," "The Dolphinarium," "Stuffed," and "Bloodletting" explore humans' relationships with animals. What observations are these stories making about human-animal relationships?

9. Endings work to make meaning of stories. Discuss the various endings in these short stories and explore their various meanings.

10. Numerous characters in this book are longing for escape. What do you think it would take for the protagonists of each story to find happiness?

11. The stories throughout this collection are told using different styles: surrealism, magical realism, realism, allegory, and social satire. Identify the style or styles of each story and explore how these various styles work to tell each particular story.

# Acknowledgments

---

This book could not have been possible without the help of so many people.

A special thanks to everyone at West Virginia University Press, including Valerie Ahwee, Jason Gosnell, Sarah Munroe, and my editor, Abby Freeland.

Many of these stories were revised during my time as writer-in-residence at the Annenberg Beach House in Santa Monica, where I finally had a room of my own.

To the editors and guest editors of the literary magazines who first chose my stories for publication: Soma Mei Sheng Frazier, Roxanne Gay, Benjamin Goodney, Daniel Handler, Sidney Sheehan, Robert Stapleton, Jessica Wickens, and Nicole Wilkinson.

The following friends contributed crucial details and expertise: Dr. Lisa Dabby, Matthew Ehrmann, Jennifer Kagan, and Albert Mikulencak.

Thank you to my University of British Columbia crew for their wisdom, which has extended well beyond our time in Vancouver: Jason Brown, Jessica Block, Zoe Stikeman, Joel Janisse, Carey Rudisill, Laura Trunkey, and Matthew J. Trafford, my very own dream team.

Thanks to my friends and family, especially to my mother, Sheila Clark, for her keen eye for grammar and punctuation.

This book would not exist without guidance from Zsuzsi Gartner, brilliant writer and dear friend.

And thank you to Basil, Peter, and Phoenix, for absolutely everything.

# About the Author

———

Jennifer Caloyeras is the author of two young adult novels: *Urban Falcon* (2009) and *Strays* (2015). Her short stories have appeared in *Booth*, *Storm Cellar*, and other literary magazines. In 2016, she served as the writer-in-residence at the Annenberg Community Beach House in Santa Monica. Jennifer holds an MA from California State University–Los Angeles and an MFA from the University of British Columbia. She teaches at the UCLA Extension Writers' Program and lives in Los Angeles with her husband and two sons. Learn more at www.jennifercaloyeras.com.

CPSIA information can be obtained
at www.ICGtesting.com
Printed in the USA
VOW03s2125310817
7163LV00003B/3/P